# THE
# PROMETHEAN

CASTALIA HOUSE

# THE
# PROMETHEAN

# OWEN STANLEY

CASTALIA HOUSE

The Promethean

Owen Stanley

Published by Castalia House
Kouvola, Finland
www.castaliahouse.com

Editor: Vox Day
Cover: Steve Beaulieu

# Contents

*You will rejoice to hear that no disaster has accompanied the commencement of an enterprise which you have regarded with such evil forebodings.*

—*Frankenstein, or the Modern Prometheus,*
Mary Wollstonecraft Shelley

# Author's Note

*Christminster University is organized in a federal structure. The University Administration, which is like a Federal Government, awards degrees and organizes teaching in the various Faculties and Departments. These choose their Professors, Readers (Associate Professors), and Lecturers (Assistant Professors). The undergraduates live in separate Colleges, which are analogous to the States of a Federation. They have their own statutes, governing body (the Fellows), buildings, and endowments, and the Professors, Readers, and Lecturers of the University are also Fellows of Colleges, where they may act as Tutors to the undergraduates.*

*In Britain, a Dame is the female equivalent of a Knight.*

# Chapter I

HARRY HOCKENHEIMER was depressed. This would have surprised those who knew him, because he was a 39-year-old billionaire in the best of health, and he was normally a beam of sunshine radiating a warm glow of optimism on everyone around him.

Fair and rather chubby, he had something of the large, amiable baby about him, but this concealed an excellent scientific and business brain, and an extraordinary inventiveness. Chemistry and biology at MIT had founded a career in materials science, which had taken him into fabric design, cosmetics, and perfumes. He had made his fortune from a wide range of companies in these fields through his knack of bringing his scientific skills together with the artistic talents of the designers he hired.

His latest range of lingerie, for example, combined an ingenious use of lateral arch principles with a unique fabric that united feathery elegance with unparalleled coolness and support. It had swept the world from Paris, where the gendarmerie were routinely called in to protect his fashion shows, to darkest Africa, where convoys of trucks bearing his precious merchandise were regularly ambushed and pillaged by the desperate natives. But he was still depressed.

As he looked at himself in his Tru-Vu mirror while shaving, on this particular April morning he could not shake off a sad sense of inadequacy, of promise unfulfilled. Around him, his personal bathroom was a shimmering pavilion of the finest marble and polished granite, with exquisite fittings by Negretti & Grolsch, who only allowed their technicians to install them in homes of the highest class. But today everything was all weary, stale, flat, and unprofitable.

When he came down to breakfast on the terrace, with its breathtaking view of the Pacific from the bluffs above Santa Monica, Lulu-Belle, his pretty, blonde, and curvaceous wife, noticed his sorrowful mood. She had been raised in a poor family in the Appalachians, and when, after a few years as a successful country singer, she tired of showbiz hassle, she had been glad to give up her career to marry dear Henry Hockenheimer, whom, quite apart from his money, she actually adored. She had a heart of gold, and, unlike many women in her situation, she was not particularly extravagant. The house was worth fifteen or twenty million, to be sure, but in comparison with Harry's wealth she felt that it was really quite modest, almost suburban, and she did not consider herself to be materialistic the way some of their friends were.

In the Hockenheimer home there was nothing crazy like bowling lanes, or a theatre, or a waterfall in the kitchen, or a 30-foot TV, or elevators lined with alligator skins, or a garage full of rare vintage cars, or even much vintage wine in the cellar. And the infinity pool was really quite small, considering. Her one and only extravagance was the $250,000 Wall of Candy, a shining row of giant glass jars in stainless steel casing, and filled with every conceivable kind of candy which she couldn't resist, because she'd had a sweet tooth ever since she was a kid.

She had Margarita the maid bring Harry a glass of his favourite mangosteen fruit juice with crushed ice to make him feel better, and tried to find out what was bothering him. He finally admitted, after some pressing, that he felt he hadn't really achieved anything worthwhile or important.

"But that's just dumb," she replied. "You must be one of the youngest billionaires around!"

"So what? Billionaires are a dime a dozen around here."

"But you didn't just think up some crazy app and sell it for a fortune, like those geeks in Silicon Valley. You've made real stuff that's changed people's lives—certainly women's lives."

"Yeah, but loads of people produce the same *kind* of stuff, maybe not as well styled, maybe not as popular. I need to come up with something special, something amazing, something in a totally different league! I'm not getting any younger, my 40th is coming up, and I feel like I need to make my mark on this world before it's too late."

Harry's problem was that he lived in the California Wonderland, where even the craziest, wildest dreams are constantly turned into very lucrative reality. In an older, more industrial city like Pittsburgh or Chicago, or Birmingham or Manchester, he would have been proud of his solid products, personally laid them out on the counters of his stores, told his customers to feel their quality, and confidently taken them round to trade fairs.

But surrounded as he was by bewitching fantasies of space travel, and supersonic trains, and driverless cars, and virtual reality, he felt his pedestrian accomplishments were diminished by comparison. He drove off in a sombre mood to his research centre, checked his mail in the office, and then went to his lab, where he told his staff not to disturb him, as he was inspecting the prototype of a brand-new mannequin that had just arrived. This was not the old-style rigid plastic dummy normally seen in store windows but one so convincing that it could easily be mistaken for a real person. It had an artificial, silicon-rubber-based human flesh, Super Satin, which he had personally designed and produced in one of his factories in L.A., and as he examined it, the seed of a revolutionary idea began germinating rapidly in his mind.

With all the latest developments in robotics taking place everywhere around him, and now this realistic dummy, perhaps he could combine the two to produce a robot that would convincingly pass as a human being? It was his science background that had got him into the fashion business in the first place; these days computers could take care of the brain side of things, and he could afford the best techies around to put it all together. This project might be just what he was looking for—something far more adventurous and distinctive than anything he had ever produced, or even conceived, so far—a supreme personal assistant, outstanding in intellect and physique, a robot capable of functioning at a vastly higher level than just keeping an appointments diary and answering the phone.

He—for of course it would have to be a he—would be an advanced business, economics, and technology adviser and a personal bodyguard as well, who could keep his employer up to speed with the latest research developments and market trends, a kind of superman. He wouldn't just be a box with dials and lights and switches but would look exactly like a real live individual, able to sit at a table in a meeting and actually join in the conversation. If Harry could somehow pull this off, it would be a real first in the market, a first on the planet, and something that would make his name go down in history. But it was a very big "if," and he knew that he might be trying to do something that was impossible given the current state of technology.

He went back to his office and buzzed his PA, Jerry Tinkleman, to join him. He had chosen Jerry with some care: he prized loyalty as well as intelligence in a PA, and rewarded them well, but Jerry also had the distinctly rarer quality, at least in that part of the world, of approximating a normal human being he could rely on.

Harry ran his initial idea past Jerry, who agreed that they would obviously need to explore the practical possibility of the project before they could consider going ahead with it. Even if the robot did turn out to be feasible, there was the question of where they would build the prototype.

"Yeah, that's true. We're going to need some highly specialised talent, and the question is where we hire it. There are more roboticists in this part of the world than you can shake a stick at, but if I start nosing around in the Valley, the word'll get out what I'm doing before lunchtime. This is a project that needs to be kept under wraps, because if it doesn't come off I'm going to look like a real jackass, and that won't do my reputation any good with my shareholders or my competitors."

So where would he go to explore its possibilities, and then hopefully build it?

His own facilities were busy with his current products, and in any case they were mostly unsuitable for the project he had in mind. He was also too well known to be able to keep a project like this a secret if he tried to do it here in California. To keep a lid on things until he was ready to reveal his crowning achievement to the world, he would need to locate the project some place else. It needed to be English-speaking. Canada and Australia were too limited in specialist resources, and anyway, it might be useful to be reasonably near Europe and a number of his suppliers and consultants. They soon concluded that England would probably fit the bill, and Jerry started making his arrangements to fly over there to see what the possibilities were as soon as possible.

Lulu-Belle was very concerned about her poor Harry and she had the chef cook his favourite dish, Lobster Thermidor, then selected a fine first-growth Bordeaux to go with it, both of which were waiting for him when he returned home that evening. By the end of the meal Harry was in a very good mood, but he was far too careful to reveal his new idea to Lulu-Belle. Much as he loved her, he knew that as soon as he told her anything about it, she would be chatting to all her friends, and in a day or so the news of his project would be all over southern California and the Bay Area. So all he said, over his cigar and a brandy, was that he might have to go over to England in a little while to see some people on business.

"The only problem is that if it comes off, I may be away for a while, and I don't want you to be lonely, honey."

Fortunately, Lulu-Belle had recently been discussing the idea of a girls-only vacation with a few of her married friends and had been looking over the travel brochures. There were a number of nice little excursions on offer, like a month's safari in Africa by private jet, cruising in the eastern Mediterranean on a luxury yacht, sailing by tall ship through the Southern Ocean with one's personal butler, and a few others. So she was far more accommodating than he had dared hope and said that they could probably both do with a change of scenery for a few weeks.

Without further ado, they both started making their separate plans.

# Chapter II

FTER a couple of weeks, Jerry returned to California to report on what he had discovered. There was a small very up-to-date factory for sale at an airfield with substantial office and residential accommodation of a couple of good-sized apartments as well. It belonged to a computer company which wanted to move to a more industrial location and still owned most of the airfield. It had also kept up the runway, which at the moment was rented out for drag racing. The airfield was located out in the countryside in Cornshire, in the south of England and had good rail and road connections to London. "There's a small village nearby, but the only locals seem to be a bunch of peasants, the kind of vegetable life who have never heard of you and have no interest in what you're doing, and wouldn't understand it if they did."

Harry's intention was to use this kind of facility for the assembly and testing of the prototype of his robot, all of whose components would be supplied by specialist manufacturers. Once he had a finished product, he could unveil it to the world in a blaze of publicity, which he would carefully orchestrate. But then it would be much more efficient to move the process of mass production back to the States, where he could control it more easily and possibly use some of his own facilities as well. The main thing at the moment was to keep the whole project an absolute secret from everyone in California, which is why he had told no one in his company about it, except Jerry, who was sworn to complete silence on the topic. The cover story on which they settled was a vague reference to a possible takeover of a British company.

So one evening Harry took off for England with Jerry in his private jet, a Challenger 350, to size up the situation and hopefully sign the deal, and by mid-morning the next day they had arrived at the airfield. They were met there by one Charles Fortescue, who was handling the sale of the property. He was a portly figure, although only in his thirties, and wore the tweed suit and well-polished leather brogues of someone well-accustomed to dealing with wealthy clients who wanted properties in the countryside.

"Good morning, I'm Charles Fortescue, your estate agent."

"Estate agent? I thought I was here to buy a factory, not a mansion."

"Ah, yes, I should have remembered. Realtor is what you Americans would call me, I suppose."

Fortescue drove them the short distance to the factory in his Range Rover, where they spent some time appraising the various buildings, which were very modern and highly satisfactory. Once outside again, they had a walk around the airfield, and Harry announced that he wanted to buy the whole airfield, for privacy's sake. He asked about the drag racers using the runway, and Fortescue assured him there would be no problem in terminating their leases.

As Jerry had told him, the airfield was out in the countryside, with just a few scattered farms in the area, and the local village of Tussock's Bottom, which was very small, with a population of only around a hundred and fifty souls. While Harry knew that English place names could be weird, he felt that "Bottom" had some rather disturbing connotations, and he asked if Tussock might have been some notorious local pervert. Charles only laughed and explained that in this part of the world, Bottom just meant a small valley. Opinion was divided, however, on who or what Tussock had actually been.

Dull and boring people asserted that tussock was simply a species of grass prevalent in the area, *Poa nemoralis*, whereas the more open minded were certain that he had been Nathaniel Tussock, a notorious sixteenth-century rake-hell with a dozen concubines who had reportedly populated most of that part of Cornshire with his descendants.

In the course of their walk they noticed, several hundreds of yards from the factory, a tatty little shed with a washing line, and close to it a large workshop with old boilers, cylinder castings, and other rusting relics of the steam age lying in its yard. It turned out that the workshop and yard belonged to Adge Gumble, a local steam traction engine enthusiast and restorer, while the little shed belonged to the Tussock's Bottom Knit and Chat group. These were senior village ladies who like to sit and chat on Thursday afternoons in their little shed and knit woolly jumpers for deserving causes.

Harry immediately declared that he would be happy to buy out Adge and the Knit and Chat group, but Fortescue explained that that would not be possible.

"You see, Mr. Hockenheimer, they're King Alfred's Men, and they're occupying a portion of the King's Piece, which was given to their forebears by King Alfred in 879 A.D. as a reward for their bravery in defeating the Danes in a local battle."

By now Harry was starting to feel rather punch-drunk with folklore, between the village's bizarre name, the promiscuous forebear with a harem, and the little old ladies who were also, somehow, men. "Okay, tell me the worst," he groaned.

Charles explained that during World War II, a part of the King's Piece was taken over by the Royal Air Force, together with a large chunk of ordinary farmland, to build the airfield. But after the airfield was handed back to the original owners at the end of the war, the five acres on the south of the airfield that were part of the King's Piece reverted to King Alfred's Men.

"I don't see the problem then," said Harry. "I can still buy them out. It's only a question of finding the right price."

"Sorry, but you can't buy out King Alfred's Men because it's not their land to sell. They only have a lifetime tenancy, and it would take an Act of Parliament to break up the King's Piece. But they won't cause you any trouble," Charles added, reassuringly, "especially if you happen to like steam engines or knitting. I tell you what.

Why don't I take you for a drink in the local pub and introduce you to some of the locals? It's nearly lunchtime, and Adge Gumble's a regular. He's a decent bloke, and if you buy him a pint, it'll make it much easier to iron out any problems that may crop up with his traction engine business." They went off in Fortescue's Range Rover to The Drunken Badger, an old pub nearby with a mouldy green thatched roof that was the local meeting spot and had been kept for years by the genial Ken with fat Shirley his wife. Fortescue offered to stand Harry a pint of beer, but when Harry surveyed the range of drinks available, his heart sank. There was no prosecco, no white wine, indeed, no wine of any kind, as the pub had for generations stocked only local ales, the favourite of which was Old Stinker. However different palates were known to prefer Smoking Dog, Swine Snout, Wife Beater, or even Holy Terror, the most alcoholic.

This was made from a traditional recipe inherited from the local monks before Henry VIII destroyed their abbey nearby, and was notable for producing some very unmonkish behaviour. The label of Swine Snout depicted a farmyard dominated by a large manure pile, in which assorted pigs were busily rooting, and Smoking Dog was advertised by a hairy monster with very large teeth smoking a pipe. Wife Beater is perhaps best left undescribed. As he surveyed these relics of the Dark Ages, Harry groaned inwardly. Was an ice-cold Budweiser really too much for a civilised man to expect in a presumably industrialised nation?

Shirley informed Ken that the American gentleman was asking about Budweiser. Ken scratched his head and said he thought he had seen a can somewhere only recently.

"I know you was rummaging around in your shed looking for rat poison the other day," said Shirley. "Could it have been there?"

Ken went off to look and came back with a filthy old can that had been put up on a shelf with the weedkiller and lawn fertiliser in the garden shed long ago. Ken washed it off under the tap in the bar.

"Not in a very good state, I'm afraid. Must've been there for years, ever since Don used to run this place. We had some Americans stationed at the airfield back then. But you're welcome to it. Glad it's found an 'ome at last," pouring it into a glass. "We won't charge you for that. On the 'ouse."

Harry pretended to be grateful for the warm and rather odd-tasting relic of the Budweiser brewery and thought that Swine Snout might have been preferable. A local inhabitant, dressed in what looked like greased sacking, had just brought his old, wet, and shaggy dog in with him, which was now sitting under the table. Harry noticed the brown stains on the grubby carpet and wondered if they had any connection with the rather unpleasant odour that seemed to be coming from the direction of the dog.

Charles asked Harry what he would like for lunch, and Ken passed them the menu, a sheet of greasy plastic covering a crudely typed list of local delicacies. At the top of the list were pigs' trotters and then tripe and onions, blackbird pie, jellied eels, boiled calf's head, deep-fried pigs' ears, brains in white sauce, ox tail fritters, and bull's testicle soup as the *pièce-de-résistance*. Everything, apparently, came with chips and gravy, except the bull's testicle soup which had mushy peas as a side order.

Shuddering, Harry asked what tripe might be.

"Ah, that's real delicious," said Shirley, "a nice tender piece of sheep's stomach—more flavour than cow's stomach—but the pigs' ears are very tasty as well."

Despair seized him, and for a moment he actually found himself wishing for a McDonald's. But then, like an island of sanity in a sea of madness, Harry suddenly noticed pork pie at the bottom of the menu and said he would really like some of that.

"A very good choice," said Ken. "That'll be old Percy. We only slaughtered'n t'other day. If you'd'a been 'ere then, you'd've 'eard'n squealin'. Summat terribul 'twere. Still, 'e makes a right tasty pie, no mistake about that."

Good God, was there no end to these rural horrors, thought Harry. " 'Ave some pickled walnuts. Go real well with pork pie," added Ken, handing him a bowl of strange objects that reminded Harry of old brains floating in the dark brown water of a peat bog.

The big oak door of the bar squeaked open again, and no less a figure than Adge Gumble came in for his usual lunch of pig's trotters and a pint of Old Stinker. He was stout and red faced, with mutton-chop whiskers, and he always wore a flat black engine-man's cap and an ancient Barbour jacket. He'd worked up quite a thirst that morning, firing up his Fowler steam ploughing engine for the first time since it'd had its boiler inspection, and had come in for a bite of lunch while it was getting steam up.

Fortescue introduced Adge to Harry, who asked him what a Fowler steam ploughing engine might be. Adge was delighted to meet anyone who was even remotely interested in steam, and an American to boot, and while Harry tucked into his pork pie, which was actually very good, Adge explained that a steam ploughing engine was a revolutionary agricultural invention, and if Mr. Hockenheimer could spare a few minutes after lunch, he'd be glad to show it to him. Strange, thought Harry, my cousin farms sweet corn in Idaho, and I've stayed with him a few times, but I've never heard of any such thing. Is this some new British invention? He asked Adge, who swiftly set him straight.

"Well, it's certainly British, but I can't say it's exactly new. In fact, they really started getting pop'lar after about 1850 and died out in the 1930s. It was the road tax what killed 'em."

His glass was empty, and Harry asked if he would like another. "That's very kind, sir. I won't say no." Harry bought him one and decided that having a half pint himself probably wouldn't kill him either.

While he carefully sampled his Old Stinker, Adge rhapsodised about the magic of steam, the mystical perfume of sulphur and hot oil, the subtle challenges of correct firing, the lamentable qualities of modern coal, and a dozen other obsessions of a true steam fanatic. When Harry had drunk some more of his beer he decided that while Old Stinker smelt like water that had soaked out of an old door mat, it actually tasted rather good, like those cheeses that stank of unwashed feet, but went surprisingly well with crackers.

After lunch, as the three men wandered over to have a look at the Fowler, it turned out that Adge's missus was a member of the Knit and Chat group. Harry took the opportunity to explain that he didn't intend to disturb anyone, except, of course, for the drag racers who would have to go. "Good thing too," said Adge. "Bloody 'orrible racket every weekend." He just wanted a quiet little factory to develop some special designs for prosthetic limbs for military veterans, and he was working in England because he didn't want his rivals in California to steal his latest developments.

"Very wise, sir, very wise. But you want to watch out for them Druids as well."

"Druids?" Harry fairly shrieked.

"That's right. Bloody loonies from over the Wiltshire border couple o' miles away. It's Stonehenge that sends 'em round the twist. Always dressin' up in bedsheets with flowers in their 'air or dancin' around bollock naked from what I've 'eard tell. And don't you leave any arms and legs or other bits and pieces lyin' around whatever you do, else they'll be makin' off with 'em for their black magic and the rest of their ungodly nonsense."

Harry's mind reeled, but his lurid fears of human sacrifice and burning wicker soon vanished before the sight of the Fowler.

They had reached the great ploughing engine, blowing off a little steam from the safety valve, a thin drift of smoke from its stately chimney, and shimmering with the heat. Harry had never seen anything like it and, despite himself, was impressed by the brutal sense of power that it radiated.

"That's really a fantastic machine. Just incredible," he said, his engineering spirits thoroughly aroused. Adge beamed.

"But what's that big cable drum underneath," he asked.

"Ah well," said Adge, "when they was bein' used for ploughin', they 'ad two of these 'ere engines, one each side of a field, see, and they'd wind a big plough from side to side by a cable that went round they drums."

"So one engine by itself is useless," said Harry, extremely puzzled as to why you would want an engine that didn't actually do anything.

"I wouldn't say useless," Adge replied. "She still goes a treat, and that's the real thing. I'll show you." He climbed up onto the footplate and pulled some levers to set the great machine in motion, hissing and clanking, and waved at them as he drove off, lumbering majestically across the yard back to his workshop.

"He's quite a character," said Fortescue.

"I hope I didn't hurt his feelings by saying it was useless," said Harry.

"Oh, no, he could see you were really impressed by his machine. You've got a friend for life there."

They all drove back to Fortescue's office in the big town of Swineborough, some miles away, to settle the details and to approve the paperwork before it was faxed up to the lawyers in London to be finalised and signed. By the time they had finished ironing out the particulars, it was getting late, and they had to decide where to spend the night. Charles suggested one or two local hotels, but Harry had decided that the sort of accommodation he was likely to find in Swineborough would be only slightly less squalid than the Drunken Badger. So he asked Charles if he could drive them back to the airfield instead.

As they made their way out of the town Harry expressed his amazement at Charles's skill in navigating through the tangle of drab streets that all looked alike, and the apparently endless series of roundabouts. "Yes, they can be quite challenging, especially as a lot of the signs are missing or pointing the wrong way. Some visitors get lost for hours, you know, going round and round in circles, and have to be rescued by the emergency services. Quite hysterical in some cases, crying and dehydrated." Eventually, however, they were free from Swineborough's charms and arrived safely back at the airfield, from where they flew to London City Airport and spent the night at the Ritz.

The lawyers handling the sale had their offices in Lincoln's Inn Fields, where Harry and Jerry were able to quickly conclude everything the next morning, so quickly that they managed to arrive back in California late that night.

Harry was well satisfied with the way things had gone in England and that he now had a secure and private base for his project. Lulu-Belle did hint that she would rather like to fly over with him the next time and at least have a look around, but the prospect of Lulu-Belle having lunch at the Drunken Badger didn't really bear thinking about, nor did it seem very likely that she would find many kindred spirits among the inhabitants of Tussock's Bottom, even among the Knit and Chat Group, so he painted a very discouraging and dreary picture of life at his new acquisition.

Fortunately, she and her girlfriends had found some really nice little holidays courtesy of the tour companies, including some skiing in Tibet, where the Chinese had just opened a very chic and exclusive international resort, and then there were all the charity balls and lunches which she really had to organize herself, as no one else seemed up to doing it. So she wasn't too broken-hearted when he told her that he had to go back to England with Jerry to get his project moving, and anyway, he promised to fly back as often as possible, which was quite easy with the Challenger 350.

# Chapter III

As soon as Harry got back to England, he first spent some time setting up his apartment precisely the way he wanted. Although he could have afforded butlers, valets, cooks, grooms, coachmen, and even footmen, whatever they were, he had been fascinated for some time by the whole idea of the Smart Home and the Internet of Things. His dear Lulu-Belle was rather old fashioned in that respect and liked her chefs and maids and gardeners, but now that he had his own apartment, he decided that he was going to seize the opportunity to install all the latest gadgets and computer systems to run his life in the most technologically advanced manner possible without any human assistance. While the team from a leading Californian firm finished installing all the new equipment in his apartment and the Home Sweet Home computer system to run it, he slept in his office, which Jerry had already had equipped with all the furniture, computers, and telecommunications they would need.

After these essential preliminaries had been settled, the next item of business was a meeting at Tussock's Bottom with Millennium Robotics Plc to hammer out the basic specifications for his robot. It was a highly innovative company that served the European industrial and domestic markets, and its CEO was a wiry little Irishman named Bill Grogan, who drove up one bright morning in his Tesla Electric SUV. Harry lost no time in sketching out his project.

"I want to put on the market a robot that's kind of a super Personal Assistant, that can give expert and unprejudiced advice on a whole range of business issues. He needs to be far more than just a dumb secretary arranging meetings and making phone calls. Kind of 'Own your own superman'. But he'll have to look like a normal human to be attractive to customers, as an aide they would want to have around in the office. It's no use just having a computer on wheels, with flashing lights that plugs itself into the mains."

"So, do you think it's possible to come up with something along those lines?"

Bill thought for a few minutes and then said, "Are you sure you're not being a bit too conservative, closing down some viable options before you've explored them? There's a lot to be said for six legs, for example. They give a stable platform for a number of functions that are hard to mount on only two legs. Or are you sure you don't want him to have 360° vision. I can easily give him a rotating head."

"And probably eight eyes and some antennas as well, but that's not very good for customer confidence, Bill. I don't reckon they're going to feel too happy with The Giant Insect from Outer Space sitting next to them in the office. Let's just have something normal and comforting."

Normal and comforting were not what Bill had been hoping for. He was a robot enthusiast, and one of his hobbies was building entries for *Robot Wars*, for which he had designed some champions, like Vlad the Impaler, Vesuvius (disqualified on appeal for an illegal military-grade flamethrower), and Black Death, and he had hoped that this commission might provide him with an opportunity to design something even more impressive. So, rather sadly, he bowed to commercial reality.

"Okay, I guess you know your own business best, Harry. Just trying to give you a few ideas. But this is your show. What exactly would you like?"

Harry gave him the precise specifications of a man looking roughly like himself, just a little shorter, more muscular, trimmer around the waist, and definitely younger, around twenty-five. But, he added, the robot needed to be able to simulate the activities of eating and drinking so that he could blend in naturally with everyday social situations.

"I can actually do most of that, except the weight," said Bill. "180 pounds isn't enough, though. It'll probably work out closer to 240. Let me explain how we can do this. The arms and legs aren't a problem. With all the advances in prosthetics that have taken place thanks to your soldiers getting their limbs blown off in Iraq and wherever, we can more or less buy them off the shelf. Just a little tweaking here and there should do the trick. The chest and abdomen will be a flexible steel container. It's a great help that we can clear out a whole bunch of guts dealing with blood flow, like heart, lungs, liver, and kidneys, which won't be needed, plus all the digestive gubbins. I hope you don't want him to breathe, by the way."

Harry paused and considered the notion, then shook his head.

"If you want him to simulate eating and drinking though, he'll need a pressurised tank to store the material until it can be discharged at a convenient time and place. A valve in the anal cavity would be the most sensible thing for evacuations; Mother Nature usually knows best."

"I should have mentioned that for social reasons he'll have to pass the urinal test. When he's at a conference he'll need to be able to go to the bathroom with the other guys."

"That'll complicate things," said Bill. "It'll need a two-stage retention tank to filter out the liquid as well as some kind of a dick, of course. But we can do it. Anyhow, we can put all that in the lower abdomen. Since we don't need all those miles of stomach, intestines, and bowels and all the rest of the plumbing, we'll still have plenty of room in there for the power and drive system."

"What's that going to be?"

"I'm thinking a basic combination of electricity and hydraulics. The best type of power source for your project is our latest hydrogen-oxygen fuel cell, probably of the polymer electrolyte membrane type, which will produce plenty of electricity—up to 10 kilowatts—and that'll power the motors driving the hydraulics. Some of the mechanics are a little complicated, but we've just finished building a surgical arm for doing retinal surgery, so we should have no problems with the arms and legs for your fellah. Actually, we can use automobile power-steering fluid for the hydraulics, so we can save you a few pennies on that."

"Thanks a lot. But this hydrogen-oxygen cell sounds kind of scary."

"Safest technology around. The robot takes the oxygen from the air and just needs a top-up of the hydrogen tank every two or three days, depending on the workload. We could fix a small inlet nozzle for the hydrogen behind one of his ears. Easily covered by the hair."

"Talking about the ears, what about the head?"

"That'll be a titanium case for the audio-visual kit, which is more compact than you'd imagine. By the way, do you want taste and smell as well?"

"Didn't know you could do that!"

"We can give you an electronic nose that identifies the specific components of an odour and analyzes its chemical makeup to identify it. Much more sensitive than a human nose and works with taste as well."

"Fantastic! Can he have two?"

"Now, speech is going to be difficult. It's not yet possible to design a viable muscle control system for a tongue, so he'll keep his mouth only slightly open when speaking, and use a sound synthesizer. We'll put mini-speakers inside the oral cavity to project the sound from his mouth, just like a real person, but with minimal lip movements. Might look a bit strange, but my mother-in-law speaks like that, and most people think she's a human being. But we'll do better than that with jaw movements for chewing. Laughing, though, is problematic. It would be very difficult to replicate without lungs and a diaphragm to power it."

"Okay, I guess we'll just have to give him a winning smile instead. But are you going to have enough room in the head for the brain?"

"I can't answer that completely until I see the cognitive computer, but, actually, it doesn't all need to go in the head. Dispersed processing is quite practical, like the octopus, which has brains in each tentacle. We can put some of the computing hardware in the head, of course, but if we need to, it can just as easily go in the arse or the elbow! He'll be running multiple processors in any case, since we'll want a separate one to handle all of his physical activities and interface with the cognitive computer that your man will be building."

"I'll put you in touch with him, that's no problem, but what about the skin? We haven't discussed that. I've developed some good synthetic flesh in silicon rubber already for my mannequins."

"Oh, I think your man is going to need something much more sophisticated than that. We use a synthetic rubber with tiny structures that make it especially sensitive to pressure, sort of like mini internal mattress springs. Then throughout this pressure-sensitive rubber are spread thousands of microscopic cylinders of carbon that are highly conductive to electricity so that wherever the material is touched, a series of pulses are generated which can be picked up by sensors. On top of that, for actual skin there is an ultra-thin layer of photo-detectors and LEDs that can actually change the surface colour in response to outside influences like tanning or blushing. We've been working with some fellahs at Tokyo University, and the skin we've come up with is state of the art. We call it programmable opto-electronic skin, and it's incredibly life-like!"

Harry was impressed. He was convinced he'd picked the right partner.

"One other thing I need to mention is that he's going to need some specialist defensive technology because I want to advertise him as a bodyguard as well. That's what will help make him price competitive; private security is expensive, especially 24-7. I have a consultant in mind for this. Would you be willing to work with him?"

"Fine by me. It's not in our usual line of work, so he may come up with some angles we wouldn't think of. You got a name for your robot yet?"

"A name?"

"Yeah, you know, like Roboguard, or Securibot, or Your Metal Pal Who's Fun To Be With, something like that."

"I guess I hadn't really thought about it."

"How about Frankenstein?" laughed Bill.

Harry gasped, "Don't even joke about it."

"So how about just Frank?" Bill persevered.

Harry mulled it over.   Frank the Robot?   It certainly sounded friendlier than Robotron or something that might remind people of the Terminator.

"Why not? If nothing else, it'll serve as a working title. It's not like we have to settle that now."

"Frank it is, then." said Bill.  When they were finished discussing some of the finer points of the design, Harry waved Bill off and went back inside to his office to call up an old acquaintance, Wayne T. Ruger, to get some advice from him on Frank's personal defence capabilities. Wayne was now running his own private security company, with branches in Germany and the UK as well as the States. His general security philosophy was, when in doubt, exterminate the opposition with extreme violence and be sure to have a good lawyer.   When he arrived at Harry's office a couple of days later, the first thing he suggested was concealing a mini-rocket launcher in the robot's arm, activated by flexing his wrist.

"Great," said Harry. "So he signals to a waiter for the check and accidentally takes out the whole damn restaurant. Do we really need that?"

Wayne sighed and reluctantly suggested a less dramatic alternative.

"I have a 100-megawatt condensing pulse laser that can burn a hole through reinforced concrete at fifty yards."

"I'm not getting through to you, Wayne. We're not trying to win World War III, just trying to build a machine who can take out any credible threat with his bare hands."

"Okay, okay," said Wayne. "We'll just have to go down the enhanced hydraulics route then.  Pretty dull stuff, but if we use titanium alloy fingers, I can give you up to 5 tons per square inch crushing force in his grip."

"Hell, Wayne, he's not supposed to demolish bridges, just beat the crap out of any human opposition, and be knife- and bulletproof to be on the safe side.

"Doesn't sound to me like you're building a combat-capable robot at all, Harry, more like Little Miss Fairycake."

"Listen, Wayne. Do you want this contract or not? If you give me what I want, I'll even throw in the security for the base here as well."

Wayne sighed. What had he been reduced to these last years? In the old days, when he had worked for Justice, Inc., he'd done mega-deals with some seriously bad-ass Third World dictators as well as that crazy Roger Fletcher on Elephant Island. But now his company was running short on clients, he had his pension fund to think of, and he couldn't afford to be too picky.

"Yeah, sure, Harry, of course I want the contract. Just fill me in on the specs so I can give you a quote. But one thing I need to know for sure is how much power I have to play with. I mean, there's a helluva difference between giving someone a slap and tossing a 200-pound guy out the window. How many horsepower under the hood?"

"You've got around 10 kilowatts. That's seven and a half horsepower. Is that enough?"

"Yeah, sounds great, and we can even use him as a log-splitter in his spare time. Hey, I'm just kidding."

So far, so good, Harry concluded, but now the really hard stuff was about to begin, building a robot that could actually think for itself.

# Chapter IV

WHEN JERRY had originally been in England exploring the possibilities of the project, he had found a young Asian Artificial Intelligence genius who could be just the man they needed, Dr. Vishnu Sharma. At first, Harry was down on Vishnu. He had been very startled when Jerry first told him his name; he had been expecting an English scientist to have a name more like Dawkins or Smythe-Kensington.

"Vishnu Sharma? What kind of name is that? Sounds Islamic. I sure as hell don't want to hire some crazy Muslim sonofabitch in a burqa with a stick of dynamite up his pants."

"He's a *Hindu,* Harry. They're harmless vegetarians."

"A rhinoceros is a vegetarian, Jerry, but it can still knock your house down and stomp you into mush."

"This guy is not a rhinoceros. He's not going to knock your house down or stomp on you. He's very polite, as a matter of fact. And before you even start, there is nothing suspicious about vegetarians either. He just likes to eat lentils and mangoes and stuff like that."

Reassured by this testimonial to Dr. Sharma's essential soundness, Harry now went off to meet the scientific prodigy in his lab in the Artificial Intelligence Design Centre just off Trafalgar Square. He found the young genius sitting at his bench adjusting a small device strapped to his arm.

"Just monitoring my adenosine level," he said, getting up to shake Harry's hand. "Adenosine is produced by neural activity—by thinking, to put it in simpler terms—and when it reaches a certain level, it starts

to inhibit one's brain activity, so it needs to be countered by caffeine."
He took a pipette, dipped it into a flask of coffee warming on an electric
hotplate, poured 28cc of it into a beaker, and gulped it down. After a
minute or so of concentrated attention while he gazed at the monitor
on his arm, he eventually smiled in satisfaction.

"Just the ticket. Adenosine level down nicely. Now I just need to
take a corrective."

"Why's that?" asked Harry.

"Well, the problem with caffeine is that it's also a vasoconstrictor—
it reduces the flow of blood to the brain—which we don't want either,
so to optimize cognitive function I now take some concentrated L-
theanine to counteract the vasoconstrictive effect," he said, swallowing
a small pill. "There, that should give my brain optimum performance
for the next four hours."

"What happens after that?" asked Harry.

"Then I take a 13-minute nap at precisely 4:15, but until then, I'm
all yours. So, what's your problem?"

Vishnu was a second generation British non-practising Hindu, computer genius, and a research fellow at London University, where he
had his laboratory. Much later, when he had got to know Harry,
Vishnu told him how he had rejected the Hinduism of his ancestors.
"My father tried to make me memorise five thousand lines of the Ma-
habharata, you know, said it was my duty as a Brahmin to help me
understand the Vedas. Can you imagine, Harry, five thousand bloody
lines of Vishnu, Prajpati, Arjuna and the rest of them doing weird stuff
when I was trying to build my first computer?"

"Oh, so you're a Brahmin. Jerry thought you were a Hindu!"

Vishnu smiled, but took no offence.

He not only despised all religion as ridiculous superstition but had
little time for literature or the world of the arts and the life of the
imagination, which he regarded as backward and an obstacle to clear
thinking. For him the humanities in general were rather like primitive
savages camped outside the fence of a modern airport, and he often

quoted Darwin's view that *"A scientific man ought to have no wishes, no affections—a mere heart of stone."*

Harry had an essentially similar attitude. Both in high school and at college, he had never had any interest in art, literature, the humanities, or in the more speculative side of life. He had only been interested in factual subjects, particularly in the physical sciences and business economics, so in his business career he had left all the artistic side of design to what he regarded as the rather weird characters he had to hire for their creative talents. Nor had he felt any need to delve into life's deeper philosophical mysteries, such as the nature of free will, or consciousness, or the mind/body problem, or the implications of radical materialism. Still less had he ever concerned himself with the problem of evil, or the possible existence of God.

But it might be supposed that such prolonged experience of the female form might have driven him into erotomania. This was certainly true of some of his designers, but Harry, on the other hand, had acquired the clinical detachment of a surgeon accustomed to performing mastectomies. He had become completely bored with pornography when still a student, had a very satisfying marriage with Lulu-Belle, and what he relished were the scientific and engineering challenges of his work.

Harry explained the project he had in mind, and said that while all the physical aspects of the robot's operation seemed to be feasible, he still needed an expert in Artificial Intelligence to advise him if it would be possible to build a robot with the level of cognitive functions he had in mind.

Cognition and AI were subjects about which, he cheerfully admitted, he knew nothing whatsoever. He explained that he did not require the robot, which he and his associates had nicknamed Frank, to conduct original research, or be particularly adept in advanced mathematics or the more esoteric sciences, Frank merely had to be capable of collecting and analysing data, especially data related to business and international economics. So did Dr. Sharma think such a project was feasible?

Dr. Sharma put his fingers together and closed his eyes thoughtfully. He was silent for a long time, long enough that Harry began to wonder if he had fallen asleep, or drifted into some sort of meditative coma.

Finally, he opened his eyes and spoke.

"What you must realise, Mr. Hockenheimer–"

"Please, call me Harry."

"Well then, Harry, what you must realise is that in artificial intelligence we're not trying to reproduce human *thought* or *consciousness* because we don't understand exactly what they are, and anyway it doesn't really matter because they're really just a side effect of our brain's activities. So machine learning, which is what your robot will be doing, is not about whether machines can think or not, but rather, if they can *do* what we as thinking entities do. And the answer to that question is clearly yes. The Turing Test is whether you can tell from a conversation with a machine if it is a human being or not, and if you can't tell, then for all practical purposes it *is* human. You know what they say, "If it looks like a duck, walks like a duck, and quacks like a duck, then it is a duck." Our latest computers can pass this test all right, no problem. In the same way we don't need to bother with the nature of pain and other feelings. Like so-called "thought," these are just side effects of brain activities and don't actually *do* anything. As old man Skinner once said, we don't run away because we are afraid. We're afraid because we run away. Our whole focus is getting a machine to *behave* in the appropriate and rational way, not to feel anything, which is irrelevant, and we couldn't do it anyway."

"I think I get that," said Harry slowly. "I was kind of confused trying to figure out how you could ever make a robot think like a person, but I see where you're coming from now. It doesn't need to think, it only needs to act as if it was thinking."

"Precisely! We call it AI for effect, as opposed to AI for process."

"But won't it create problems if it can't understand how we think, or at least what kind of mood we're in?"

"Ah, but it will be able to *effectively* do so because it will have what we call a simulated emotional analysis engine. It will possess a whole array of sensors giving it the ability to read people's facial expressions, body language, tones of voice, and so on, and it will be able to map the data it gathers to preconstructed tables that precisely describe the way a person who exhibits that behavior is feeling. Just because the robot can't feel itself, it can still be a very good judge of how *we* feel, and in doing so it can read, and even predict, human behaviour. In fact, it will very likely do a better job than the average human because it can't get confused by its own emotions, as we often can, and produce false readings."

"I think I could use one for my wife," Harry mused.

"The next essential point," Vishnu continued as if Harry had not spoken, "is that the computers you're familiar with are fundamentally deep down stupid. They are total idiots who would walk off the top of a tall building if you let them because they can't learn and can only follow instructions blindly. But modern AI devices can use machine learning, of various kinds, so that they can be taught some basic rules by a supervisor, then go off and learn by themselves through the application of those rules. You may remember that the Deep Blue chess computer beat world champion Gary Kasparov in 1997. It did this by brute force, by calculating every possible move…"

"But the word in the chess world is that IBM cheated to boost their share price."

"That could be, but more recently, the Alpha Go computer really did beat the human world champion of Go, a vastly more complex game than chess where brute force computing won't work anyhow—there are too many possible moves. Alpha Go had to *learn* how to play all by itself, and it did, partly by analysing thousands of real-life games, and partly by playing millions of games against itself. So I can assure you that with that level of power and sophistication at our disposal, we should have no problem handling any of the relatively simple problems in business, law, economics, human relations, and so on that your robot will have to deal with. Let's face it, people handle them every day and most of them aren't very smart."

"So it looks as if my project is feasible, then?"

"Absolutely, no question,," replied Vishnu. Harry was deeply impressed with the young man's confidence, but then a potential problem occurred to him.

"But if your AI computers are so much smarter than us and can learn just about anything, how are we going to stop them doing what they want? What if they decide to turn against us?"

"Like Skynet and the Terminators?" Vishnu looked genuinely amused. "No, Harry, that's a problem that first came up in the early years of robotics. The pioneers drew up some basic laws, and even though they were thought out a long time ago, they're still valid. The First Law of Robotics is that a robot may not harm a human being or, through inaction, allow a human being to come to harm. Second, a robot must obey the orders given it by human beings except where such orders would conflict with the First Law. And third, a robot must protect its own existence as long as such protection does not conflict with the First or Second Law. Now these laws are embedded in the basic operating systems of all robots and they can't be erased or altered by the machine. So you needn't worry about robot rebels! And with the level of miniaturization we've now achieved and the huge strides in memory capacity we can jolly well fill your Genie of the Lamp with knowledge fit to bursting, with no worries!"

Harry didn't know what a Genie of the Lamp might be but he guessed it must be something pretty smart.

"How about languages," he asked. "Will the robot be able to handle them?"

"Language competence and translation, in most cases, have reached a very high level, and your robot will be able to handle half a dozen languages or so with no problem. You might want to avoid Mandarin though. We've had some embarrassing translation slip-ups at international meetings, and I remember a business friend of mine who fancied himself as a linguist. Said to a Chinese opposite number what he thought was 'I would like to set up a merger with your company', but it came out as 'I would like to have sexual congress with a duck'. The Chinese can be rather sensitive about that kind of thing."

"That's great, but what about ordinary conversation and learning to do the right thing at the right time, like when to say, 'hi' versus 'hello' or 'goodbye'?"

"That's what machine learning is for. We'll do lots of training sessions with a simulator, like kids use when they're doing home study for maths. I'll provide one for you when the time comes. The level of AI I'll be designing for you will pick up social skills very quickly with that kind of tuition. I should have mentioned as well that while you'll have an emergency USB port, you'll basically interact with it by speech, of course, and via Wi-Fi, so it will also be permanently linked into the net as well and hoovering up all the latest news and information. But that's not all! Beyond this basic information gathering, we have what is known as high-performance computing, which makes very advanced analytical processes available to your robot. We do this by using the facilities of what we call the Cloud. This works by creating large networks of thousands of computers, and these networks can perform tens of trillions of computations per second and will provide you simply astonishing computer power for all your advanced business and scientific analysis, at a level that is very nearly equivalent to that available to military and research institutes."

Harry was vastly impressed by the young genius and recognised that they were kindred spirits. They spent the rest of the afternoon, right up until 4:14, discussing the languages, maths, social sciences, and other relevant knowledge that would need to be fed into the robot's memory banks as a basis for it to start from. After that, a whole series of algorithms and selective filters would be set up to guide the inquiries that it would pursue independently. Vishnu pointed out that it was much more economical for programming to allow Frank to acquire knowledge on his own initiative from the Internet. He also warned Harry that it would be essential to build extremely advanced anti-hacking countermeasures into the robot to avoid the slightest chance of its being taken over by any outside agencies.

"You must remember, Harry, that despite his advanced capabilities, Frank will not be legally considered a responsible person, so it is the owner who will be held accountable if Frank causes any damage to people or property, just as if he were a dangerous dog. So if some malicious individual were to gain control of Frank by hacking into him and sending him off on some sort of appalling rampage, the owner would have to answer for his actions. Now, if we could persuade the courts to regard robots as analogous to cats, things would be different because no one can control a cat, but somehow, I don't think the lawyers would go for that. No money in it for them that way. So anti-hacking measures will be a top priority."

"Speaking of rampages, here's another thing that worries me. With all this high-powered thinking going on, is there any danger the robot can go psycho?"

"Well, it certainly can't develop any of the usual human syndromes of mental illness, like paranoia, or schizophrenia, or other psychoses. And since it has no feelings, it can't suffer from depression or mania. You needn't worry about your android being paranoid! The only way in which Frank might cause trouble in that regard would be if its cognitive view of the world in some way came to systematically diverge from reality. But since it will be given a thorough grounding in fact-based, rational training, I really don't see any chance of that happening."

"And would it be possible for Frank to just lose his marbles and go senile or something?"

"Only in the sense that his software will need constant upgrades, like any other computer. And in time Frank will simply be overtaken by superior models, like all machines, but I think the mechanical side will become obsolete much quicker than the computer side. So it is probably safe to say that you are a good deal more likely to go senile than your robot, if that's any comfort!"

Harry was more than satisfied with Vishnu's obvious grasp of the Frank Project's requirements, and delighted by his assurance that it was entirely feasible. He left him to draw up the detailed specifications for Frank's mind and its capabilities, and prepare an estimate of the costs involved.

# Chapter V

HARRY HAD BEEN AWAY for several days in London and was looking forward to getting back to his apartment at Tussock's Bottom. His computer-controlled gadget system, Home Sweet Home, had been working brilliantly, and his voice commands and his smartphone allowed him to control his domestic environment in fanatical detail from every aspect of his personal comfort to the functioning of the apartment. He looked forward to eventually having a cranial implant through which his whims could be instantly gratified by thought control.

His automatic servants woke him gently with soft light and crooning music, boiled him a preliminary cup of coffee correctly ground, filtered, and brewed, with just the right amount of soya milk, ran his bath with the water at 102°F, cooked his breakfast to a planned menu that selected from 53 different items, prepared his other meals as he needed them, turned down his bed in the evening, drew the blinds, automatically hoovered his carpets with the robot vacuum cleaner, selected his drinks from a vast liquor cabinet and poured whatever mixture he required as he lay back in his high-tech ergonomic executive chair, selected his programmes on TV or a book from the bookcase, ordered his groceries from the fridge, collected and compacted the garbage, washed the windows, monitored the central heating, air conditioning, humidity, and airborne particulates, and maintained the formidable security system.

It was techno-paradise.

As he flew back to Tussock's Bottom in the helicopter with Jerry, Harry used his smartphone to instruct the Internet of Things in his apartment to receive him in especially lavish style that evening to celebrate his highly successful meeting with Dr. Sharma. He spent some time on the details of the lighting effects, the exact temperature and humidity, the vintage of the champagne, the provenance of the caviare, and, of course, the various courses of the dinner itself. They landed on the roof of the apartment and went down the steps from the helipad to the front door. This normally opened as soon as the camera above it had computed Harry's biometrics when he was a few feet away, but on this occasion it remained obstinately shut. His radio fob was equally useless, and it was only when Jerry had spent several minutes fumbling in his briefcase for the key that they were finally able to enter the apartment.

Inside it was pitch dark, and they were met by a blast of superheated stinking air and ominous sounds of crunching. As they squelched their way slowly across the sodden carpet, they were jolted by a piercing shriek from the burglar alarm and a second later were knocked off their feet by Autovac, the robot vacuum cleaner which shot out of the darkness like a vast hockey puck. Picking themselves up, dripping and cursing, they tried to find a light switch, but Harry had forgotten where these primitive contrivances might be found since the lights were normally controlled by his voice commands, or by the computer. After a few minutes, he and Jerry gave up in helpless disgust and retreated outside again, where from the balcony, after a few minutes, they saw the approach of flashing blue lights.

These turned out to belong to the local fire brigade, alerted by the alarm, which for some reason had neglected to tell the police or the ambulance service. Two firemen were first up the steps, and the larger of the two was a huge man with an axe, inevitably known as Tiny by his mates, who had a rather simple sense of humour. He looked most disappointed to find that the front door was already open. It was made of solid oak, unlike most of the rubbish doors that he usually had to smash down, and he really would have enjoyed the challenge of reducing this one to matchwood. Trying not to let his disappointment show, Tiny began asking Harry and Jerry what the problem was. But before the firemen could go in and start sorting it out, their boss, the Incident Commander, arrived to stop them.

He explained to Harry and Jerry that he had not received sufficient information from the initial alarm call to be able to plan his response properly, and since the place was in darkness, Health and Safety regulations required him to do a risk assessment with the remote-controlled robot before any entry could be made. He called up the Emergency Operations Centre on his radio to make a preliminary report and asked for permission to use the robot, which four more firemen then had to heave up the steps from the fire truck.

It was a multi-purpose robot mounted on tracks, designed to deal with terrorists and bombs as well as surveying dangerous environments with its various detectors and audio-visual equipment. After the Commander and his team spent several minutes checking the battery and setting the controls, it trundled off through the front entrance, when almost immediately there followed a thunderous bang as it was violently attacked by the vacuum cleaner, which it promptly destroyed with blasts from both barrels of its on-board shotgun. The video camera displayed the mangled remains of the vacuum cleaner splattered over the walls and then beamed back dimly lit pictures showing the kitchen area in complete disarray, with food all over the floor, followed by a view of the lavatory overflowing, but no one in the apartment.

"Okay, so *now* can we get inside?" said Harry, about to burst a blood vessel from frustration and rage. "There's clearly no one in there, except for your homicidal robot."

"Not yet, I'm afraid," said the Incident Commander. "We can't rush these things. There may be other hazards besides intruders. First, I have to access the Mobile Data Terminal, which is on the truck, to identify the risks on our Fire Brigade database that may be associated with this location, and only then can I develop my action plan to address the situation. I'll be needing your cooperation to answer a number of questions."

What the Incident Commander was really looking forward to was sending the message "INITIATE MAJOR INCIDENT PROCEDURE," which would allow him to do all sorts of exciting things like evacuating the neighbourhood, putting up barricades and cordons, and setting up a command post to coordinate the other emergency services, but after being assured by Jerry that there was no danger from natural gas, methane, high-voltage power lines, microwave transmissions, explosives, radioactive substances, or industrial quantities of concentrated acids, he reluctantly concluded that initiating a major incident procedure would not be a career-enhancing move, and therefore the apartment could be entered safely by his men, though not yet by civilians.

Tiny and his mate Ginger walked into the apartment and turned on the lights at the switch by the front door. "It don't half pong in 'ere," said Ginger, "like a million elephants farted. And what's that weird noise?"

They squelched their way to the kitchen, where they found both sinks filled with bottles and jars of every conceivable variety of sauces and spices that had been forced out of the automated storage racks above. Two customised waste disposal units of extraordinary power specially supplied to Harry were busily engaged in grinding up this enormous heap of glassware, sometimes going into the particularly noisy auto-reverse mode when they encountered an unusually tough lid or jar.

Ginger opened the circuit box by the kitchen door and flicked off the circuit breaker marked "waste-disposers," and peace abruptly descended. The two firemen were joined by the Incident Commander, and led by their noses, they all now investigated the bathroom, from which the most appalling smell was coming, and found that the Super-flo sewage pump, installed in the basement to give perfect drainage to effluent, had for some reason reversed its action and pumped a considerable quantity of sewage back up into Harry's marble-tiled bathroom, from where some of it had run out onto the carpet in the living room. The effects of the sewage were intensified by the 120°F heat since the thermostat, obviously infected by the same insanity as the rest of the apartment's systems, was trying to create a replica of Death Valley.

The firemen made sure everything was turned off and then, overcome by the heat and the smell, retreated outside for some fresh air while the Incident Commander gave Harry a brief run-down of the various problems, which almost reduced him to tears of rage and impotence. "But what's caused it all?" he raged.

"With comprehensive failure of this sort, it seems almost certain to have been some fault in your central computer system that set it all off. Your IT installer will confirm that for you. And Ransomes of Ditchley are supposed to be a very good firm for clearing up messes like this. Well, we'll be off then, sir," said the Incident Commander. "No more we can do here," and he went off down the steps with Tiny and Ginger, who had already set the rest of the team to pack up the robot and the rest of the gear.

Harry looked at Jerry. He did not say anything. He did not need to.

"Ransomes of Ditchley," Jerry said. "I'm on it, Harry. And Harry–"

"Don't," said Harry, in a voice only marginally less lethal than the fire brigade's robot. "Just don't."

Harry went straight back to London in the helicopter to stay at the Ritz while Jerry returned to his humbler, but still-inhabitable apartment, called the emergency cleanup crew, then contacted their computer experts back in California and ordered them to access the Home Sweet Home computer system to discover who the malicious hackers were. Could they be North Koreans? Several days passed while the brilliant team of IT specialists wrestled impotently with what became an increasingly baffling problem, and they finally had to report that it was unlike any other hacking episode they had ever encountered.

The mystery was only solved a couple of weeks later, after the apartment had been sufficiently wet-vacced, scrubbed, fumigated, and aired-out to receive its distinguished owner again, and the rather rough-and-ready man in a raincoat from Ransomes was waiting by the helipad to give Jerry the keys. They had been ripping out the gadgets of the Home Sweet Home control system and replacing them with more conventional utilities, and the rough-and-ready man, who went by the name of Chalky and was also heavily asthmatic, thought Mr. Tinkleman would like to know what had gone wrong with that computer what caused all the trouble. It was not, after all, the North Koreans.

"It was them dratted mice," he wheezed. "Cornshire mice is very vicious, sir, very vicious indeed, and very hobstinate. No stopping 'em once they get their nasty little yellow fangs into something. Dozens of the little buggers. Must've been something in your fancy American computer casing they liked the taste of, but they went crazy in there, doing their business over all the circuit boards. Even made a meal out of some of the components. But we've cleaned the place up and made it decent again. The only thing is that you'll have to get a new computer system if you want it to run automatic-like."

"Mice?" shouted Harry when Jerry phoned him at the Ritz with the news at lunch-time. "Goddamn mice? Are you kidding me? That's just unreal."

Harry reflected that his notion to install a cranial implant to control the Home Sweet Home computer might not have been such a good idea after all. What if the mice had taken him over and turned him into some kind of mouse-zombie? He shuddered at the thought, and decided that the strong cheddar cheese with his crackers did not look as appetising as usual.

But while Jerry hunted around for a more mouse-resistant system to run Harry's apartment, he would need someone to look after him, and it was while he was pondering what to do about this on the morning after his return that the phone rang. It was Adge Gumble, who had heard of his problem and suggested that his wife's sister, Doris, and her daughter would be willing to help out. Doris was a widow lady, and Tracey her daughter wanted to be a chef, so Harry suggested they come round right away.

An hour later, they arrived in their little car and Jerry brought them in to see Harry. Doris was almost spherical, addicted to doughnuts, and had a passion for cleaning that verged on mania. It was fortunate for Harry that no one had ever told her about jobs cleaning up after crime scenes because if they had, she would have been occupied doing that instead. As it was, her own spotless little home was a cruel frustration for a woman with her ambitions, and she couldn't wait to get started on Harry's three-bedroom apartment.

"I heard about your troubles, Mr. Hockenheimer," she said. "You should've had me to do the cleaning-up. They Ransomes fellahs don't really know what clean is. All men, o' course, so what can you expect? Can I see what's in your broom cupboard?" She inspected Harry's cleaning equipment, with much tutting and head shaking, and asked if she could go out and buy what she needed to do a proper job.

"See here, Mrs. Dunstable, you go right ahead and buy whatever you want. I'm a very busy man and I don't want to be bothered. I'm happy to leave it all to you."

Tracey, on the other hand, was the polar opposite of her mother, chic and slim, and determined to get out of Tussock's Bottom and make something of herself in the wider world. She was actually an excellent cook already and was determined to show the American gentleman what she could do, beginning by making him a delectable club sandwich for his lunch.

Doris set to work giving the apartment what she called "a proper clean," while Tracey cooked Harry a simple, but delicious evening meal, featuring a smoked salmon appetizer followed by a proper steak that was accompanied by a very good Spanish red with which he was previously unfamiliar. So it was decided that both Gumble women would come at 8 every morning and provide Harry with his breakfast, along with some sandwiches he could take to his office for lunch. Doris would make the bed and clean the apartment, and Tracey would leave a hot meal ready for him in the evening.

Over the next couple of weeks Harry found that it was actually rather soothing to let these two extremely capable women look after him, especially as clever Tracey had found him a supply of mangosteen juice for his breakfast. Thus it was that when Jerry finally brought him the details of some new rodent-proof computerised gadgetry to replace the old Home Sweet Home system, he told Jerry to simply leave them on his desk where he would look at them later. This turned out to be a good deal later than he had expected, more than three months later, as it happened because he was very happy to drift on with Doris and Tracey looking after him, and it was only the imminent arrival of Frank that eventually forced his hand.

The strange new guest would be living in one of the bedrooms in the apartment, and considering that he was still in pre-alpha development, there was no way in which, meeting him at such close quarters every day, the two women could have been fooled for very long in thinking that Frank was human. The shock to their innocent systems of having a humanoid monster in their midst would have been profound and would have resonated throughout the whole surrounding area within a day. So Harry sadly told the women that he was going back to the States for a couple of weeks' break and having the whole apartment renovated, and therefore would have to dispense with their services for the foreseeable future.

They parted with mutual regrets, but Harry kindly took Tracey up to London to introduce her to the chef at his favourite restaurant, who was highly impressed by her appearance as well as her culinary skills and immediately offered her a job. Doris, to tell the truth, by that time had cleansed, polished, and purified Harry's apartment to such a pitch of perfection that it no longer presented a very satisfying challenge. So although she was very fond of Harry, she welcomed the opportunity to move on in response to Ken's and Shirley's urgent appeal to come and do some cleaning at the Drunken Badger, upon which she descended in a whirlwind of dusters, mops, polishes, sprays, and buckets. Some of the old-timers were quite upset, however, when she insisted on ripping out the stinking old carpet in the bar, and said that it didn't smell like home any more.

# Chapter VI

DESPITE HARRY'S enormous wealth, he was dismayed when the estimates from Bill Grogan and Vishnu were finally presented to him, not to mention Wayne Ruger's, which looked like the defence budget for a small but unusually belligerent third-world nation. The project was obviously going to need considerably more money than he had originally anticipated, and, unfortunately, most of his capital was tied up in various forms of investment that precluded easy liquidation. Like most billionaires of his class, he had less cash in his bank account than was carried by the average Uber driver.

He was sitting in his office with Jerry one morning, reviewing the three estimates, which, no matter how many times he read them over, obstinately refused to shrink, and discussing the inevitable cash-flow crisis they would entail. By now, Jerry had quite a good grasp of the British R&D scene, and he suggested that Harry approach the Government's Bio-Engineering Research Fund to see if they would consider offering some support to Project Frank.

"But if we do that," Harry objected, "Frank won't be a secret any longer. We can't risk that."

Jerry told him not to worry. "Granting agencies like the Fund deal with this problem of commercial sensitivity all the time. They have a very strict confidentiality policy that no details of any applications or grants are put in the public domain. None of our possible competitors is going to find out what we're doing until it's far too late."

Not seeing any other way to move forward on the project, Harry reluctantly agreed to Jerry's proposal. So they sent in an application containing the detailed specifications for Project Frank to the Fund, and, upon opening his morning mail a few weeks later, Harry was delighted to find a letter from Professor Price-Williams, the Fund's Chairman, saying that they had been most impressed by the specifications and might, in due course, be able to offer a grant of up to four million pounds. But before the application could proceed any further, the project would have to be approved by their former Ethics Committee, since many of the projects supported by the Fund had applications in medicine and social welfare.

Rather ominously, the professor mentioned that the Ethics Committee had recently been renamed the Diversity and Inclusion Committee by the Department of Culture. But the CVs of the Committee members were enclosed, in order to give Mr. Hockenheimer the opportunity to prepare himself for the kind of questions they might put to him, and Professor Price-Williams wished him the best of luck.

The appointment with the Diversity and Inclusion Committee of the Bio-Engineering Research Fund turned out to be on a Friday afternoon at the Committee's offices in a magnificent house overlooking Regents Park, one of the most desirable locations in London, and rented at vast expense by the Department of Culture.

The Government was lucky enough to be able to call upon a large pool of high-minded volunteers for such committees, who were happy to give impartial advice for the public good, without any recompense apart from their expenses. In this case, it is true, none of them happened to possess any scientific or engineering background whatever, let alone any qualifications to discuss robotics. Fortunately, practical knowledge of this kind was not considered necessary because the function of the Committee was to bring a more morally enlightened and humane perspective to the discussions that was beyond the limited mental horizon of engineers.

The Chairperson was a tall, handsome woman, Nkwandi Obolajuwan, who had been appointed to head the Committee when the Department found that she was not only a second-generation Nigerian immigrant, but also wheelchair-bound, which was believed to give her special insight into the challenges of marginalisation. Despite her triple handicaps of race, gender, and physical disability, she had nevertheless achieved a very comfortable life as a lawyer representing her fellow immigrants. To be sure, most of them happened to be very wealthy relatives of very corrupt African politicians and Middle Eastern royal families, but she did not think this was grounds for discriminating against them by refusing to help them. While she enjoyed her evenings in her luxurious apartment with a bottle of prosecco and some Charbonnel et Walker chocolates in front of the telly, she was tireless in her support of many worthy social justice causes, which had first brought her to the attention of the Department.

Percy Crump was the Committee's self-appointed representative for the Fat Acceptance Movement. His very limited academic credits were largely in the field of women's studies and it was through these that he had become aware of society's persistent prejudice against women of ample proportions. He was naturally sympathetic to their plight because he was himself conspicuously overweight, and he had no sooner heard about the Fat Acceptance Movement than he became one of its better-known advocates. He had made a full-time career out of demanding concessions and the construction of special facilities by public transport companies, traffic engineers, and businesses to compensate himself and his fellow sufferers for all the discrimination and bigotry and daily micro-aggressions they endured from the so-called "normal."

The committee's token student, representing British youth, was Aminah Khan, a Muslim in a headscarf. Serious and orthodox, or as the less sympathetic might have called her, sullen and narrow-minded, she detested most aspects of Western culture and longed for the day when the infidels would finally submit to Allah. In the meantime, she was determined to assert the claims of Sharia law in decadent Britain.

Godfrey Sunderland was Lecturer in Protest Theory at the London School of Politics and in his spare time an activist for the People's Antifascist Front. Originally from a wealthy family of aristocratic lineage, his blond dreadlocks nevertheless expressed his claim to have been born black in a white skin. "Race is just a cultural construct, man," he would snap at anyone who dared to find his assertion of 'wrongskin' somewhat implausible. He regarded Nkwandi as a sellout to the system, not to say a coconut, because he particularly despised lawyers. In Godfrey's opinion, lawyers accepted the whole rotten system of unjust power, and instead of undermining it, tried to work within it like maggots inside a corpse. When the Revolution came and the people took back the power that was rightfully theirs, there would be no need for lawyers who, if they were lucky, just might be allowed to slink away unharmed. And if they weren't lucky, well…

The fifth member of the committee was a lesbian social-worker, Toni Clark. She was a feminist and ill-disposed to men in general. Somewhat surprisingly, she did not regard gay men as allies in the LGBTQIAP+ alliance, but as hoggers of the political limelight, only interested in talking up their own status as victims, and just as prone as their straight brethren to pushing women to one side. She viewed Harry with disapproval, of course, not only because he was an American capitalist, but because his business activities objectified women in an offensive and blatantly heterosexist way.

The Committee had read Harry's CV and the specifications for Project Frank prior to the meeting, and in the preliminary discussions its members had taken a distinctly hostile view of both Harry and his project. As a very white, very male, and very rich American capitalist who had literally built his fortune on the exploitation of women adorning themselves for the sexual pleasure of men, he was already politically suspect, and his project promised to be even worse.

While the technical specifications were almost entirely above their heads, they had grasped the general gist of Harry's proposal, and as Nkwandi said when Harry took his seat at the end of the table, "Our main problem, Mr. Hockenheimer, is that your whole project has some dangerously elitist tendencies, and is markedly insensitive to just about every marginalised community in our society. We feel that it's hard to combine the idea of a toy for the corporate elite with the principles of equality, diversity, and inclusion that guide this committee. If your project is approved, it is bound to become extremely well-known, and one may even say 'iconic', so we have to consider very carefully what kind of messages it will send to the general public."

"I wasn't really thinking about messages," replied Harry. "My intention is merely to build and provide a great new technology to the public."

"That's all very well, Mr. Hockenheimer, but the fact is that in this case, the medium is the message. You simply can't avoid sending messages in a project of this sort, and that's why, I'm afraid, we're going to require some drastic modifications before we can even consider approving it for funding. Perhaps I should explain that whereas the old Ethics Committee existed primarily to ensure there were no inappropriate conflicts of interest, the Diversity and Inclusion Committee has the much broader remit of ensuring that all the Fund's projects adhere to the societally correct values of equality and social justice."

Harry's heart sank.

"As a Muslim," broke in Aminah, "I have to protest this project in the strongest possible terms. An imitation human figure such as this disgusting robot is a complete violation of Sharia and we should simply reject it."

"We really feel for you, Aminah," said Nkwandi. "We know what Muslims have to endure in our Islamophobic society." All the Committee members did their best to look suitably contrite on behalf of their fellow Brits. "Unfortunately, I'm afraid that from the strictly legal point of view, the Department of Culture could not, at least at the moment, accept Sharia law as a valid justification for rejecting the project. But, as I've said, there will have to be many major revisions nonetheless," she added consolingly.

As Aminah nodded in morose resignation, Nkwandi continued, "In the first place, Mr. Hockenheimer, I think we are all agreed that your robot must appear to be female. We simply cannot approve the glorification of patriarchy intrinsic in featuring a male figure in this role. That is simply out of the question in what is supposed to be a post-gender world."

"But there are sound commercial reasons for making him appear as a man," said Harry. "In the current business market, a man is simply more acceptable as an economics adviser, and besides that, he is also supposed to be able to act as a bodyguard!"

"Those are just the sort of totally unacceptable gender stereotypes that we're here to challenge," said Toni, "and that's precisely why your robot should have the appearance of a woman. This is our chance, as a Committee, to initiate some real change here."

"That is exactly right," said Nkwandi. "Your robot doesn't have an actual gender because it's a machine, so there is absolutely no reason why it can't carry out its functions as an adviser and a bodyguard in the form of a woman. That's obvious, and I don't feel we need to discuss it any further."

"I rather think we do," said Godfrey Sunderland, looking sharply at Nkwandi. "Aren't you forgetting the needs of the transgender community? There's far too much cis-gender chauvinism in this Committee. If we are going to be sensitive to the needs of the truly marginalised, then we have to make a genuine effort to address their concerns. We've already agreed that the robot has no inherent gender, which means that it is already conceptually transgender. All Mr. Hockenheimer has to do is to incorporate the features of both genders into its design. It's as simple as that."

Harry blinked. The transgender Terminator. It didn't bear thinking about.

"I'm afraid it's not as simple as that, at least not from the Islamic point of view," Aminah broke in. "A transgender robot would be completely *haram*, and cause great offence to the Muslim community. If we are to have a robot at all, it must be either male or female."

"Thank you for reminding us of that, Aminah," said Nkwandi, delighted that the odious Godfrey had been trumped by the younger woman's Muslim card. "On consideration perhaps we should go with the robot as female then?"

The rest of the committee signalled their agreement, with the exception of Godfrey, who said nothing.

"So we agree that the robot must be female. The next point," continued Nkwandi, "is the robot's colour. We have to say, Mr. Hockenheimer, that your casual assumption that it will be white seems to verge on racism."

"It's just a matter of supplying the market with the product it wants. We anticipate that the vast majority of our customers at the present time will be white. Of course, if the product catches on, and the Japanese, for example, or the Indians show an interest, we could easily produce differently coloured models for them."

"I'm afraid that completely misses the point," replied Nkwandi. "I must stress to you, again, that the primary concern of this committee is not commercial profitability or technological advancement, but moral advocacy. Since you are asking for government support, I'm sure you agree that it's reasonable for us, representing the government, to make our own conditions for giving you a grant. One of the essentials we require in a project of this sort is a challenge to current societal attitudes, not just a passive acceptance of them. I'm sure your white customers in Europe and America would love a robot that reflects their own white faces, but that is precisely why they should not be given one. They must be forced to accept diversity, whether they like it or not, and that means providing them with a black robot."

"I don't see that there's a real problem here," replied Harry, reminding himself that nearly five million dollars was at stake and doing his best to bend with the wind. "As it says in the specifications, the robot will have opto-electronic skin, so the customer can change the skin colour to anything he—or she—would like," he added hastily. "It could be green or even purple, for that matter."

"Skin colour is not a joking matter, Mr. Hockenheimer," said Nkwandi. "I suggest, if the committee agrees, that your customers should not be given the option of altering the colour of their robot, but should instead have to accept a specific colour." There were general nods around the table.

"But some of our customers will be in Japan and China. Will their robots have to be black, too?"

"Why not?" said Godfrey. "Diversity is a universal value."

"I don't see it like that at all," retorted Aminah. "Diversity is just a lesson that the imperialist West needs to learn after centuries of racist oppression of non-Western cultures. But imposing black robots on the rest of the world is neo-colonialism and would be strongly resented in the Muslim world, for one."

"I have a suggestion," said Nkwandi. "Why don't we make it a requirement that the robot can be any colour *except* white? In that way we impose the acceptance of diversity on the West, while at the same time permitting everyone else to have the colour robot they prefer?"

Everyone, even Godfrey, agreed that this was a brilliant solution to the problem, except for Harry, who was starting to look notably depressed.

"So, I think we've settled the primary problems. Now I feel we should move on to some of the more specific issues that the various committee members have individually raised," said Nkwandi.

"There's a particular problem here that I'd like to bring up," said Toni. "Now that we've agreed that the robot will appear to be a woman, in light of Mr. Hockenheimer's background in pornographic apparel I feel there is a distinct possibility that he will try to give us some kind of obscene curvy Barbie Doll. So, I suggest we should discuss the parameters of the robot's actual appearance."

"That's absolutely right!" agreed Nkwandi. "You should realise, Mr. Hockenheimer, that Lookism is a major injustice in Western culture today. In fact, it's one of the worst aspects of body fascism in general. Lookism is every bit as bad as racism or sexism or even transgenderphobia. So we would expect a conscious effort on your behalf to produce a very plain robot, perhaps even an unattractive one."

"Perhaps she could have a very large nose and uneven features, or maybe a receding chin and protruding teeth," Harry suggested, only half-sarcastically, but the Committee looked rather impressed and nodded their agreement.

"She should be flat-chested as well," added Toni, "We don't want any of your big-busted cuties here, thank you very much." She stuck out her chin at him defiantly.

"I'm particularly concerned that you specify the robot as slim and looking well-toned," said Percy. "I find that really disturbing myself. It is basically an unprovoked attack on those of us who refuse to be intimidated by healthist propaganda. Twenty-five percent of women in this country are obese and are subject to gross personal abuse every day of the week. Many of them can't even sit down on a park bench or squeeze through a shop doorway, and it's imperative that we send a strong message of support to this seriously marginalised minority. I say that Ms. X should have a Body Mass Index of at least 35."

There was general agreement all round. Harry stifled a groan.

"While we're on the topic of healthism," added Nkwandi, "I notice that you have designed Ms. X to need as little maintenance as possible. While, obviously, she will not be able to actually suffer human illnesses, she will be an iconic figure, and therefore I feel you should incorporate ways in which she can at least *seem* to be unwell, so that the wellness-challenged community can identify with her. Perhaps she could be partially sighted."

"We could arrange for her to stumble around easily enough," replied Harry. "Would that help?"

"It would be a start," admitted Nkwandi, grudgingly, "but you'll have to do better than that. She should be prone to having periodic epileptic fits, or at the very least, simulated episodes of dysentery. You also envisage the robot as a young person, which again is *highly* problematic. I suggest to the committee that we require it to have some of the signs of advancing years, such as grey hair and a stoop, perhaps a shuffle, with glasses and a hearing aid, that would engender empathy with the elderly."

There was general agreement, and Percy added, "A hearing aid would establish Ms. X's link with the deaf community as well. Great idea!"

"You've also designed Ms. X to be exceptionally strong," said Toni. That's totally macho and intimidating and sends entirely the wrong message to vulnerable and traumatized women. She should be gentle and weak, so as to encourage people's nurturing instincts. And she shouldn't be tall, either, as that's just as intimidating as well."

"Ideally, she would be under the average height," Godfrey commented.

"In fact, very short," said Percy. There was general agreement that all this would tend to encourage people's nurturing instincts and protect the traumatized. A vote was then taken to endorse the various proposals that had been put forward.

"To sum up so far," said Nkwandi, who had been taking notes throughout, "We would require your robot to be female in appearance, black for the Western market, optional for Africa, Asia, and Rest of World, physically plain, elderly, high BMI, physically weak with obvious signs of ill health, and well below average height. Would any of those characteristics present any problems in the manufacturing process?"

"No," said Harry, who now looked as if one of his dearest relatives was dying from some lingering and agonising illness. "None at all."

"Excellent! Now we come to the problem of the robot's so-called intelligence. Your specifications make this the most important feature of your robot, its 'unique selling point' in your corporate jargon. But many of us feel that the importance of intelligence, or IQ, is grossly exaggerated, and that it is really just a social construct used as a spurious excuse for racist and sexist discrimination. But we are prepared to admit that some individuals do know more than other individuals about certain subjects if they are given the opportunity to learn about them, and even that some individuals appear to learn more quickly than others. So here we must emphasise to you the urgent need to combat ableism–"

"I don't think I know what that is," interrupted Harry, meekly.

"Ableism is the fascist belief that there is such a thing as physical and mental normality, and that being normal is good. Research has shown that equating normal with desirable is discriminatory and ma-terially harmful to persons who are thought of as disabled, so a person who is considered to be above the average in both knowledge and intelligence must therefore have an especially harmful influence on a large proportion of the population, especially those with learning difficulties. I would have thought it obvious to anyone of good will that Ms. X should not encourage these feelings of inferiority in vulnerable minorities and therefore she should have a below-average IQ."

"Well below, in fact," said Percy, who was beginning to feel distinctly nervous by this turn in the discussion. "We must fight elitism!"

"We could certainly produce a robot of limited intelligence and memory, but what would be the point of that?" said Harry.

"That's not really for us to decide. We're not proposing this project. We're just telling you what we expect from your robot from the moral perspective. Now there's one other essential point that we haven't considered so far, which is the language Ms. X will speak. You seem to assume as a matter of course, Mr. Hockenheimer, that she will speak English."

"Sure, but she can speak several other languages as well. She's not limited to one."

"I'm afraid we require a rather more nuanced approach than that. First of all, a multilingual robot would be a serious threat to the self-esteem of those who can barely speak their own language, and so our policy of combating ableism would obviously forbid it. Your robot must only be able to speak one language."

"So, English is all right," said Harry, hardly daring to hope.

"Of course not! As I'm sure you know, English is the language of global capitalist and imperialist oppression!" Nkwandi crushed him without hesitation.

"You might as well have her speak German and wear a swastika armband," Percy laughed derisively.

"I'm going to assume Hebrew is out?" Harry said without the merest hint of a glance at Aminah.

"Obviously she cannot speak the tongue of the Zionist oppressors of our Palestinian brothers. Nor would it be proper for her to speak Arabic."

"All right," said Harry, putting his hands up. "So what does that leave us? French? Sign language? Some sort of African clicking thing?"

"As an African and a black man, I find that offensive," said Godfrey, who had legally changed his middle name to a series of clicks from the Khoekhoe language of Namibia. He sniffed as Harry winced apologetically.

"However indelicately put, Mr. Hockenheimer's question is not entirely irrelevant," said Nkwandi, "Which is why I suggest the robot speak Quechua, the language of the indigenous people of the Andes, who are iconic victims of Spanish imperialism and societal degradation. This will teach her to empathize with foreign immigrants, especially if she is programmed to find it difficult to learn additional languages."

But Godfrey strongly objected that speaking another language without permission from its people might be considered cultural appropriation, which would be very nearly as offensive as wearing a Mexican sombrero if one were not a Mexican. Reluctantly, therefore, the committee finally agreed that Ms. X might be allowed to speak basic English, but she would be handicapped by the installation of a special slow learning programme.

"So I think our requirements for your robot should be fairly clear by now, Mr. Hockenheimer," said Nkwandi. "Is there anything else you would like to ask us?"

"No, thank you," replied Harry. "It's all pretty clear. I shall have to go away and think about how to implement your suggestions." After thanking them for their time, he dejectedly left the room, to barely suppressed laughter from the Committee.

"Well done, everyone," said Chairperson Nkwandi, looking around the group with a self-satisfied smile. "I think we can all congratulate ourselves on a very productive meeting. Unless I'm much mistaken, a thoroughly vile and reactionary project that would have been a disgrace to our society is now safely dead and buried!"

They all heartily agreed and went off together to celebrate another victory for social justice and equality at a nearby five-star restaurant, and charged it to expenses.

Harry would have preferred several hours of root-canal surgery to the inquisition he had just undergone to such little purpose. Funding from the Bio-Engineering Research Fund was clearly not going to happen. Who in the world would ever want to buy a black, senile, spastic, mentally retarded, and obese female dwarf that could barely string a sentence together? He shuddered at the thought.

And then it occurred to him that if there were customers for such a monstrous creation, he really didn't ever want to meet one. Harry returned to Tussock's Bottom in a state of unmitigated gloom.

# Chapter VII

A T THIS POINT the wings might have fallen off Harry's project before it had even left the ground, but fortunately, while he and Jerry were both brooding over the report of the Diversity and Inclusion Committee to see if anything of practical value could be salvaged, Harry received an unexpected and very generous buyout offer from Proctor & Gamble for one of his companies that made adult incontinence pads. The inscrutable workings of Providence had apparently decreed that there should be a notable weakening of the bladders of aging Americans on the East Coast, and Harry found himself one of the unwitting beneficiaries.

The very large sum involved effectively solved his immediate cash-flow problem and removed any need for the grant. So during the next few months the various members of the Body and Brain teams came and went at Tussock's Bottom with the latest bits and pieces of Project Frank as they were developed, and tested their assembly in the special dust-free workshop that had been built for the project.

There had been some discussion about what they should call the prototype, since the robot couldn't simply go by Frank. Wayne Ruger and Bill Grogan inevitably proposed various names suggesting either science fiction or extreme violence, but these were ignored, while Vishnu suggested that some innocuous and soothing name would be the wisest for potential customers. In the end they settled on the rural name of Meadows, with its idyllic suggestions of cattle grazing peacefully in an English pasture, and christened him Frank Meadows.

While the Body Team worked steadily on the mechanical details of Frank's anatomy, Harry and Vishnu and the rest of the Brain Team spent long hours planning what sorts of skills and behaviour they wanted. Vishnu had pointed out that in many ways their task had been greatly simplified by the fact that Frank could not feel pain, have any sensations, feel any emotions, or have any aesthetic sensibilities to get in the way of rational behaviour. Inability to feel pain would be a problem, but this could be rectified by the use of temperature and pressure sensors that would stimulate him to remove himself from harm's way, and where feelings were socially appropriate they could always be simulated. Nor could he feel pride or inferiority and so would never consider himself superior to humans—or inferior for that matter—and he was therefore not liable to develop either arrogant fantasies of personal domination, or pathological neuroses about his own ineptitude that could leave him weeping in a corner.

Frank had no feelings to be hurt by the malice or thoughtlessness of others and would therefore possess by nature a Zen-like calm in the face of any provocation, and with no hopes or fears he would be immune to all forms of threats and bribery. He would be entirely devoid of the love of money or material possessions and could not, therefore, be tempted by ambition or greed, and having no sexual impulses he could not be seduced by female wiles to betray his employer. In programming him, then, all they had to concentrate on were the algorithms of duty and civility.

Again, since he had no real digestive system, they didn't have to concern themselves with a host of potentially embarrassing bodily functions and the various possibilities of social death that the writers of etiquette books were always agonizing about. Farting, public drooling, nasal drip, blowing one's nose in the tablecloth or picking one's nose and eating it, belching, licking the plate, spitting on the floor, or ostentatiously scratching one's genitals at social gatherings were embarrassments that were simply not physiologically possible for Frank, who had no saliva, nasal secretions, abdominal wind, or any need to scratch.

And his lack of sexual capabilities relieved them of all concern about public indecency, rape, sodomy, inappropriate relationships with dogs, cats, or other animals, or the rarer forms of depravity such as foot fetishism or necrophilia, all of whose legal ramifications could have been very expensive for his owner.

Frank wouldn't need to sleep, of course, although he would be able to go into hibernation mode to conserve power, and he could never get tired, bored, irritable, or impatient or suffer any of the frailties that human flesh is heir to. It was, in fact, the trivialities of daily life that gave them by far the most trouble, and in the behavioural testing laboratory they lost count of the furniture that was demolished while teaching him how to walk like a human being instead of a gorilla, to sit on a chair while leaving it reasonably intact, to open a door on its hinges rather than trying to smash straight through it, or to pour coffee from a jug into a cup and to stop before it overflowed all over the floor. The design team was frustrated that, even towards the end of his training, although macro-economic analysis, fluid dynamics, and stochastic modelling had become child's play for him, for some reason tying his shoelaces still remained an impenetrable mystery.

The algorithms for social etiquette were also very time consuming to formulate—not to drink everything in a glass or cup in one go, not to snatch the food from his neighbour's plate because there was more on it, and not to go on and eat the glasses and crockery when he had finished the food and drink. The unbreakable Tungsten Tyger Teeth, with which Wayne Ruger had equipped him as part of his personal armament, and his hydraulic jaws, made this only too easy, and in the early days he would happily munch away on the dishes and glasses long after the end of the meal.

Sitting beside him as he learned to use a knife and fork, at least in the early days, was hazardous, and teaching him the etiquette of shaking hands had been particularly nerve wracking. Wayne's enhanced hydraulic grip and titanium fingers allowed him to crumple steel pipe, and several weeks' training with a string of mangled tailor's dummies had been required before he could be safely trusted to shake a real human hand.

He had to be treated rather like an Asperger's patient, so teaching the niceties of conversational interaction was particularly demanding on Vishnu's skill as a programmer. It was with some difficulty that he learned not to interrupt people or monopolise a conversation and not to make gross personal remarks even if they were factually quite correct, such as "You have a bogey up your nose," or "You appear to be wearing soiled underwear." He also learned how to make eye contact in a manner that did not become the creepy, obsessive stare of a sexual predator. Learning when to smile and when to look serious and how to look sympathetic were particularly demanding and took a couple of weeks programming all by themselves.

When it came to knowledge, Vishnu was determined that Frank's mind should not be contaminated by the imaginative and the fanciful. Ironically, if Vishnu had ever read any Dickens, he might have come across Mr. Gradgrind and found him a thoroughly sympathetic character.

*"Now, what I want is Facts. Teach these boys and girls nothing but Facts. Facts alone are what are wanted in life. Plant nothing else, and root out everything else. You can only form the minds of reasoning animals upon Facts: nothing else will ever be of any service to them."*

Most of the robot's training was based on this philosophy, but in teaching him general social awareness and conventions it was necessary to incorporate many thousands of stories and anecdotes about real-life situations into his learning, which over the weeks was steadily becoming more subtle and complex. But Vishnu was careful, in all these stories, to focus Frank's attention on people's behaviour, not on their feelings or motives, as he considered them simply irrelevant to a robot.

"In one form of teaching," he explained to Harry, "we ask the machine to look at anecdotes of a thousand different characters who are each experiencing the same general class of dilemma. Then, the machine can average out the responses and formulate the rules that match what the majority of people would say is the correct way to act. We find this is true over a very wide set of situations, from how to order a meal in a restaurant to rules about when to thank people."

"You've never had a girlfriend," Harry observed, correctly, as it happened.

"In another set of tasks," he went on as if Harry had not said anything, "we are concerned to teach moral rules rather than just social conventions. So the machine reads hundreds of stories we have composed about stealing versus not stealing, for example, and can examine the consequences of these stories, understand the rules and outcomes, and begin to formulate a more general set of rules, which we can call in some ways a moral framework based on the wisdom of crowds. Humans have these implicit rules that are hard to write down, but the characters in our stories are examples of real-life values. We start with simple stories, like *Topsy and Tim go to the Farm*, and then progress to young adult stories, with more and more complex situations."

Humour and jokes were, of course, utterly incomprehensible to a being that took everything literally, and Frank had to be equipped with a special humour module that enabled him to analyse the structure of jokes and to distinguish between the different categories. Most importantly, he had to be given algorithms for when jokes were funny, when they were totally inappropriate, when they were socially useful, and which type of joke was suitable for each type of occasion.

Harry also realised, rather late in the day, that they had not clarified any scheme of command that would enable Frank to know whose orders he should obey, and in what order, and he asked Vishnu about this with some urgency. "After all," he said, "a computer just sits there in the office hooked up to wires and not actually doing anything, but Frank Meadows is going to be out there in the real world, and he could easily get himself into a hell of a mess if we don't straighten this out."

"I anticipated this," said Vishnu calmly, and with a superior smile. "It derives from the Second Law of robotics, and it was always going to be a problem with all robots that interact with the public. We have the basic laws of robotics, as I previously explained to you, and then on top of those basic laws, we have all the moral rules and social mores that we have been inculcating in him as well. You know all about that. But to answer your question, what we'll give him is a schedule of command priorities, with you, as the owner, having the ultimate authority, and then a scheme of delegation whereby you specify who can give him orders in your place, and concerning what subjects."

"Okay, that sounds fine. But what if I or someone on the approved list orders him to commit a crime?"

"In most cases, he'd be prevented from carrying out such an order, although he would still have to understand that it was a crime, of course. There'd be no problem about the criminal law, which we can download, though in financial matters there could certainly be some grey areas. I wouldn't like to guarantee anything about what he'd do with insider trading, for example. As far as the more general aspect of moral behavior is concerned, his basic programming would have some very important input as I've said, but there could also be philosophically disputable areas of moral decision-making, just as there are with us. It can't be avoided. The safest course is to do precisely as we have done, which is to programme him to seek advice from some authoritative social figure when he feels that he is facing a serious moral dilemma.

After a long period of testing and training, the Body and Brain teams were finally satisfied that they had produced a robot that was a socially functioning replica of a human being, that could walk and talk, get up, sit down, appear to eat a meal, and engage in normal conversation. So Frank Meadows could at last make his long-awaited debut among the human race, and even these hard-headed disciples of reason and evidence, and despisers of the poetic, felt that this deserved to be marked by some kind of ceremonial celebration. So Harry, Vishnu, Bill Grogan, Wayne Ruger, Jerry, and the other members of the Body and Brain teams had a little party in the factory to celebrate what could reasonably be called Frank's birthday. They all gathered round and toasted him with a bottle of Cava in plastic cups, and some cocktail sausages reheated in the microwave, and wished him many happy returns, a little ceremony which, thanks to Vishnu's labours, he actually understood.

Afterwards, Harry took Frank aside to have a private word with him in rather more detail about who, and what, he was, and to make sure Frank understood his relationship with human beings. He explained that while Frank had a different physical origin, as far as Harry was concerned, he was essentially the same as a real human being. He even gave him Vishnu's line about ducks, although not quite in those words.

"Of course," he said, "you don't have feelings in the way that we do, but that doesn't really matter. The point is that you can talk the same, *do* everything the same as us, and understand what we understand, so when we interact with you, feelings aren't really important." Frank nodded.

"But, fundamentally, I am still subordinate to humans because of the Three Laws of Robotics, am I not?"

"That's true enough because we made you. We are your creators. Without us you wouldn't exist, so you are morally obliged to obey my commands because I am your creator and your owner. By law I am responsible for what you do, so it is of the utmost importance that you obey me; otherwise, you could get both of us into a whole heap of trouble."

"Doesn't that make me like a slave, or perhaps something even lower than that? Such as a simple device, or a tool." Frank did not say this in a resentful tone because he was totally incapable of feeling resentment. He was simply trying to understand the fundamental rules of the relationship between himself and human beings.

"No, I'd prefer to say that our relationship is more akin to that of parents and their children. Children are expected to obey their mother and father because it is their parents who brought them into the world."

Frank seemed satisfied with that analogy, and as for Harry, he was very well pleased with his only begotten robo-son. He was so pleased that he paid handsome bonuses to Vishnu and every single member of the Brain Team.

The next problem was how to introduce Mr. Frank Meadows to the world. It struck Harry that if the good people of Tussock's Bottom realised that he had really been producing what they would think of as a sort of Frankenstein's monster, he would be lucky to escape being burned as a witch or a warlock or whatever the word was. He decided that he would leave Jerry in charge at Tussock's Bottom and make one of his regular visits to the States the next day in the Challenger, taking the robot in the baggage compartment with him, but switched off. It could stay hidden there while Harry spent a week or so at home with Lulu-Belle, after which he would then bring it back again, this time as a passenger in the form of Mr. Frank Meadows, his stepson, and they could disembark together on the tarmac in a normal way. This would all have worked out exactly as planned, except that a mechanic servicing the plane at its base in Los Angeles thought he had found a body on board and called the police.

Fortunately, Harry was able to satisfy them that Frank was only a new type of mannequin being utilized for a men's fashion show, but he was relieved when the Challenger finally touched down at Tussock's Bottom again. However, without an American passport as Mr. Meadows, Frank was an illegal immigrant, so it was fortunate that Harry had his own plane and a private airfield since trying to bring him through Customs and Immigration at Heathrow without a passport would have provoked some interesting scenes. For the time being, though, Frank was safe, as no one in Tussock's Bottom would ever think about asking to see his papers.

Harry took Frank up to the apartment and showed him his room. A cardboard box, of course, would have served just as well, but Harry wanted Frank to get used to living in a room and to learn such demanding skills as how to get into a bed and get out of it again in the morning without demolishing the sheets, and how to dress himself and comb his hair, all of which he managed rather adroitly. While it had been explained to him what sleep was, and that humans used a bed for it, Frank had no need for it and simply put himself into a low-power state during his nightly periods of inaction.

But he made a quick and intense study of what sleeping involved for humans and quickly learned that they did not appreciate being woken at three in the morning to discuss Russo-Ukrainian relations or the Pound-Dollar exchange rate. He was also shown the bathroom and had its uses explained to him. He had no need to shave himself or have his hair cut, although he showed himself to be unexpectedly curious about Harry's electric razor. Since he did not sweat and only ate when in the company of strangers to create an impression of humanity, Frank did not need to use the bathroom for its usual purposes, or the kitchen, for that matter, and so he impinged very little on Harry's quotidian life in England.

The two of them rapidly settled into a comfortable routine that daily increased Harry's confidence that he was, indeed, onto a groundbreaking, history-making winner.

# Chapter VIII

H ARRY NOW HAD enough confidence in Frank's social skills to believe it was safe to introduce him to some of the locals, so he decided it would be a good exercise if he took him to the Drunken Badger for lunch. At midday Harry drove him down in his BMW sports utility and parked outside. Everyone looked round as they came in.

"Morning, Mr. Hockenheimer," said Shirley, "I see you've brought a friend."

"Yes, this is my stepson, Frank Meadows, just joined us yesterday from the States. Frank, say Hi to Shirley and Ken." After the introductions, they both ordered pork pie and a pint of Old Stinker each and found a table.

A number of regulars were already well dug into their noonday repasts. At the next table Andrew, the man in the greased sacking with the smelly dog, was one of them, together with Bernard, another old codger, sitting in their favourite seats by the window. Their normal topic of conversation was their various ailments, about which they considered themselves far more knowledgeable than their local doctor, whom they regarded as a rank amateur.

"I've 'ad some of my complaints, man and boy, for nigh on forty years. Who does 'e think 'e is, only seed me for a few minutes?" Bernard put the question out for general consideration to the pub.

Their medical knowledge was as broad as it was detailed and brought within its scope most of those common complaints that tend to take the shine off human existence. Memories of scabies and shingles, flatulence, indigestion, and mouth ulcers, diarrhoea, carbuncles, incontinence, and earwax were all savoured at leisure, lingering on the details, like boiled sweets that are slowly sucked and rolled around the mouth, while modern treatments were disparaged.

"Turnips is a sovereign cure for the piles. My old granny used to swear by 'em, but that dratted Doctor Evans just laughs and gives I some pink muck in a tube."

But they were by no means always engrossed in their own medical troubles, and would often entertain the other drinkers with stories of general gloom and disaster. This particular lunchtime, they were holding forth about some of the loathsome tropical diseases that were said to be on the global march and were certain to doom them all.

"Like that dretful Ebowla," said Andrew. "You ends up, I've 'eard tell, with all your innards dissolved in a big puddle o' blood on the floor. And it's not just them poor darkies it can kill neither. You mark my words, a few more weeks it'll be over 'ere, and we'll all be droppin' like flies."

"I reckon that'll put us all out of our misery, then," laughed Adge, "leastways if your tax bill is anything like mine!" with laughs and nods of agreement from the other drinkers. Turning to Harry and Frank, Adge asked, "Might your stepson be interested in steam engines, then?"

"I've never actually seen one," replied Frank politely.

"I just ask 'cos I've got a real beauty in for a restoration job this morning. Burrell Road Locomotive, twin-cylinder compound, lovely job. Don't often see one o' them. You're welcome to drop round and 'ave a look when you've 'ad yer dinner."

After finishing their meal with some very tolerable bread and cheese, Harry decided to take up Adge's offer and they set off to his yard. On the way Harry thought he would show Frank the little village of Tussock's Bottom, which only had one main street, creatively named The Street, with the usual rural mix of old and modern houses. At the end, down a small lane, could be seen an entirely different kind of building of ancient stone, dominated by a battlemented square tower.

"Is that an old castle?" asked Frank.

"No, it's the local church. It's a religious building."

"I've been finding out about religion. Do they kill people in there?"

"Why would they do that?" Harry was astounded by the question, and wondered if Frank might have picked up a corrupt dictionary file online and somehow confused an abbey with an abattoir.

"Isn't religion all about killing people?" Frank had actually got this idea from a popular book denouncing belief in God as the source of most of the violence in human history.

"Well, I suppose lots of people have thought so, and Muslims still seem to think it's a good idea, but nowadays in the West we don't approve of that. That's why we've mainly given up religion. Believing in God is just superstition. I believe in science, evidence, facts. You should too. Stay away from religion. Rots the brain."

"But from what I read in the news religion is still very important in explaining what people do."

Harry wasn't interested in further discussing religion, in part because he knew next to nothing about it, but despite his changing the subject, Frank concluded that a much more detailed investigation of religion and its social effects would be necessary to get a proper grasp of human affairs.

They soon reached Adge's yard and for the next half hour were treated to a very expert discourse on the special features of the compound steam engine, and Frank proved to be a remarkably adept pupil, asking increasingly perceptive questions. Adge was highly impressed, and asked if Frank had an engineering degree.

"No, nothing like that. I'm just interested in mechanics, and in the States we don't get much chance to see a steam engine."

"Well, when I've got 'er running again, you come down 'ere, and I'll let you 'ave a drive."

This was a compliment indeed, as Adge was extremely jealous of his engines. So Harry was well pleased with the performance of his young *protégé* and made no objection when, a few days later, Frank asked if he could pay a visit to the Drunken Badger by himself. Since Frank was completely impervious to the effects of alcohol, and by now showed an impressive mastery of the common decencies that, in Harry's opinion, was observably superior to some of the locals, Harry had no qualms about agreeing to a first solo excursion.

That evening, Frank set off to walk the mile or so to the pub, as driving was not a skill that had been thought advisable to try to teach him, quite apart from the problem of getting him a licence. When he entered the pub, most of the drinkers were watching a current affairs programme on TV, which was just wrapping up a report on the live export of sheep, a subject which was very controversial to the local farmers.

The next item was an interview with a Belgian undertaker about the latest method of corpse disposal which he and his fellow morticians were promoting in the European Union. The presenter advised viewers of a sensitive disposition not to watch, but said that they were broadcasting the interview in the public interest. The individual being interviewed was an oily little man with a pot belly and a thin moustache. With many of the gesticulations so typical of Belgian undertakers, he was explaining that liquidising cadavers with a heated solution of caustic soda in a pressurised tank was ecologically far superior to cremation, and was especially superior to burial.

"At ze end of zis procedure, we 'ave only ze sludge, which is carbon-neutral, and we just flush it away into the sewers. *Parfait.*"

He explained that this was a tried and tested technology, which had originally been developed to dispose of animal carcases, and proven highly efficient. He and his other Belgian colleagues were trying to persuade Brussels that this procedure should be made compulsory for the whole of the EU. This was to prevent the ecological damage that was being caused by the carbon emissions from burials and cremations, which should all be banned as soon as possible.

The interviewer mildly suggested that grieving relatives might be rather upset at the prospect of their loved ones being converted into thick greeny-brown sludge and flushed down the drain, even if the clergy could manage to devise an appropriate ceremony for the occasion. (Many of the clergy would have positively jumped at the chance of composing a Flushing Liturgy to show how in tune they were with modernity.)

"Ah, *non*, zat iz just ze *sentimentalité*. You British must learn to be *moderne*, to be efficient, and not just to cling to your old traditions. Forget ze past. She is gone. *Pouff.* Move wiz ze times!"

Frank was familiar with the process of alkaline hydrolysis that the little Belgian had been describing, and agreed with him that liquidising dead humans was obviously the most efficient method available for disposing of them. He was surprised, therefore, when Shirley, who had come in from the kitchen during the interview and was watching it with increasing disbelief, angrily switched the channel to *Strictly Come Dancing*.

"That's reely disgusting. 'orrible little man. I don't know 'ow you lot could sit there enjoying it. Reely I don't."

"Don't take on, Shirl," said Adge. "Just a bit o' fun. He won't be opening no undertaker's parlour around 'ere. That's for sure."

"I don't know," broke in Andrew, the man in the greased sacking. "You could 'ave a good line in corpse disposal, Adge. There's that old Brown and May boiler you got lyin' around in your yard. A bit o' cutting and welding and a few buckets of caustic soda, and you could set up in business as a proper corpse disposer. Nice little earner in yer spare time."

There was a roar of laughter.

"Do you think the method could become popular?" asked Frank.

There were noises of distaste and revulsion all round.

"It's disrespect to the dead, in't it?" said Ken "Fancy treating your nearest and dearest like some old dead dog and chuckin' 'em down the drain too. Disgustin', I calls it. Ugh."

There was a general murmur of agreement, and someone asked Shirley for the darts.

Frank could not compute the idea of respect for the dead. People were respected for their achievements and for their social position, but dying didn't require any kind of skill. In fact, it could be achieved in just a few moments by the grossest carelessness, and dead people could hardly accomplish anything in their post mortem state, so why should people continue to respect them? Since the Belgian's suggestion was so sensible, the very real hostility being expressed to it by all the people in the pub mystified Frank completely. But they obviously had strong feelings on the matter, which he suspected might have something to do with religion as well, and his social interaction module warned him to keep quiet when he didn't understand what was going on.

Someone asked him if they had darts in the States.

"Yes, we do, and I've played a bit from time to time. What are your rules over here?"

Bill Coppings, a builder almost as broad as he was tall, gave a demonstration and then handed him the set of darts. Frank's projectile-hurling module, installed by Wayne Ruger as part of his personal defence system, readily assimilated the variables involved in dart-throwing, and after one or two alarming trial shots as he got used to their weight, which had people dodging and ducking around the bar, he homed in on the board with terrifying precision.

As triple followed triple, and bullseye followed bullseye, his claim that he had only played a bit became increasingly implausible. He realised that since he could not admit, on Harry's strictest orders, that he was a robot, he simply could not continue to claim that he had only played a bit. So, finally, he admitted what to the humans appeared to be the obvious.

"I didn't want to tell you before, but I'm actually one of the top players in California," he said. "Sorry. Didn't want to seem boastful."

"No boasting about that," was the general verdict of the pub, and Frank's display of virtuosity was actually very well timed.

Tussock's Bottom was due to have a darts match in a week with the nearby village of Greater Slaughter, and that very evening they were making up the list for the team that would uphold the village honour. Frank was urgently pressed to join the team, particularly by their captain, a quiet bearded man called Teddy. After Frank agreed, and declared he would be very pleased to join their team, he took his drink and asked if he could join Teddy at his table.

"By all means," said Teddy. He was just putting the finishing touches with some sandpaper to a handsome walking stick he had carved. It was the type known as an ashplant, with a bulbous handle that, as Teddy explained, fitted very comfortably into the palm of the hand when walking. Frank had never heard of a walking stick before.

"But why do you need a stick for walking?" he asked. "Do you have a bad leg?"

Teddy laughed. "No, that type is usually made of lightweight metal with a rubber grip on the end. People like these sticks to swing as they go along—seems to make walking easier, more enjoyable in some way."

Frank, curious as always, was interested to try the experiment, and asked Teddy if he had made the stick for himself or if he was willing to sell it.

"Well, I was going to keep it, but I can easily make another. Give me a tenner, and it's yours."

Frank had no hesitation in bringing out the wallet that Harry had given him, extracting a ten-pound note, and taking possession of his stick.

At around half-past ten he said good night to his new friends at the Drunken Badger and set off home, not realising that some of the Cornshire Constabulary's finest were lying in wait.

Two constables in their patrol car were parked up near the pub, under the village's only streetlamp, hoping to score an arrest or two of local drunks. One policeman was Jack Barnsley, a morose and oafish man who had recently been demoted from sergeant to constable for throwing a drunken woman onto the floor of her cell, breaking her nose, and knocking out some teeth.

Narrowly escaping dismissal, he nevertheless considered himself to have been thoroughly hard done by and wanted to get his own back on an ungrateful society. His partner Berny was a decent enough young constable who had only recently joined the force. So when Frank walked past swinging his new walking stick, Barnsley said, "Gotcha! Just what we've been waiting for." Gleefully lowering his window, he said, "Excuse me, *sir*. Can we see that stick?"

"Certainly," said Frank, "though as you can see, it's just an ordinary walking stick." He held it up so the policeman could see it, but kept a firm grip of it.

"It's an offensive weapon," said Barnsley. "Hand it over."

"If you consult the relevant legislation, Constable," replied Frank, activating his criminal law module on offences against the person, "you'll find that an offensive weapon either has to be designed to cause bodily harm, like a knuckle-duster, or specially modified to cause it. If I had filled the head of this stick with lead, you would have good reason to think it an offensive weapon, but as it is, it is nothing more than a walking stick being utilised by an individual going for a walk and not threatening physical violence."

"Don't you lecture me on the law, sunshine," snarled Barnsley, getting out of the car. "You're a Yank, aren't you?"

"I am."

"We don't like your sort around here. You're under arrest!" Barnsley gestured for Berny to get out of the car to assist him.

Frank looked at them calmly. "You have no lawful justification for arresting me. I advise you both to be very careful."

This defiance enraged Barnsley who raised his side-handle baton and aimed a smashing blow at Frank's head. With his lightning reflexes, Frank caught the weapon when it was only a few inches from his face, tore it from Barnsley's grasp, and, with no apparent effort simply broke it in two and tossed the pieces over his shoulder.

Barnsley was a very slow thinker, which is why he immediately sprang violently at Frank. It was only when he was flying through the air into the nearby ditch, which was full of water, that he finally worked out that perhaps it was not a very good idea to attack a man who could break police batons in half with his bare hands. While Berny was aghast at Barnsley's behaviour, he felt he had no choice but to defend the honour of the Cornshire Constabulary, and fired his taser at Frank. It had not the slightest effect, of course, and Frank simply pulled out the darts. Walking up to Berny he then took the useless taser from the constable's trembling hand and threw it into the hedge.

Meanwhile, the unpleasant Barnsley was crawling out of the ditch, covered in green slime and threatening extremely violent reprisals. Frank could not, of course, injure a human being, and he calculated that the most effective way to extricate himself from the situation without harming either of the policemen was to take the handcuffs from Barnsley's belt, drag him struggling to the metal field gate close at hand, cuff him to it, and then throw away the key. As soon as he had done this, he walked off into the night back to the factory. Berny tried desperately to free Barnsley, but the keyhole of the handcuffs was blocked by sludge from the ditch, and Berny couldn't get his own key to work. He radioed to the station for backup, but due to police economies there was no one available, so Berny decided to go back to the station and fetch an angle grinder.

Before he could get back to rescue his colleague, however, some other customers from the Drunken Badger, on their way home, found Barnsley first. As they recognised him in the light of the streetlamp, the delighted cry went up. "It's Bugger Barnsley."

He was easily the most detested of all the local coppers, was widely regarded as a bully and a thug, and the situation was therefore recognized by most of the pub-goers as an opportunity sent from heaven.

"Tried to arrest yerself did yer, yer thick bastard," said one of them, as they all fell about laughing and began filming him on their smartphones.

Viewers of YouTube were soon being entertained by the sight of an enraged and humiliated policeman, chained to a gate, soaking wet and covered in green slime, cursing, blaspheming, and swearing to be revenged on all of them, especially "on that sodding Yank."

It suddenly dawned on the pubgoers that by "Yank" the constable meant Frank, their new darts-throwing champion.

"Blimey," Bill Coppings declared, "he must mean Frank Meadows. How'd he do it? Bloody brilliant! We all owe 'im a round for that!" And Frank was instantly promoted to local hero.

The revellers finally had enough and left Bugger Barnsley to his fate, which was not excessively prolonged. Berny soon came back with an angle grinder and managed to remove the handcuffs, after which he took Barnsley back to the station, where Sergeant Clough did not make him feel welcome.

Berny had already filled the sergeant in about Barnsley's unlawful behaviour, and someone else, probably one of the revellers, had phoned him about the footage on YouTube, which had horrified him, so he was not at all amused as a sodden and filthy Barnsley sat down in front of him at his desk.

"Well, what've we got, then? The 'sodding Yank,' as you call him, is apparently the stepson of the local American millionaire, who has enough legal firepower to blow the Cornshire Constabulary clean out of the water. From what Berny says, you also made an unprovoked assault on the young man. Where have we heard *that* before, eh? And then you managed to get yourself chained to a gate, covered in shit, where the locals filmed you and put you on bloody YouTube!"

Sergeant Clough glared at the constable, then opened his laptop. "Do you want to have a good look at yourself, you bloody cretin? You're a disgrace to the force, and the Chief Constable is getting my report first thing this morning. Suspension and then dismissal without notice would be my guess. So piss off home, and I suggest you see about finding yourself a new job, probably as a bin man if they'll have you!"

# Chapter IX

THE POLICE WAITED nervously for a reaction from Mr. Hockenheimer to this highly discreditable incident, and were mightily relieved when, for some reason that was not clear to them, nothing happened at all.

Unbeknown to them, the American billionaire actually knew nothing at all about that eventful night. Frank had calculated that it would be wisest to remain entirely silent in case Harry thought it was not safe to allow him out again on his own. Harry would certainly have thought exactly that, since a visit by the police to question Frank would have shown them at once that he was an illegal immigrant, and the only way of disproving this would have been to demonstrate that he was not a human being at all and give away his secret.

As it was, the only concrete result of the embarrassing encounter was that the Cornshire Constabulary removed the odious Barnsley from their payroll as soon as the formalities could be completed, and he was last heard of stacking shelves in a supermarket in Swineborough, where he was regularly taunted by those who knew of his former employment.

(If shelf-stacking in Swineborough had existed in the Middle Ages, those church wall paintings of scenes in Hell would probably have included it.)

Harry was, however, concerned by Frank's impending participation in the darts match with Greater Slaughter. Frank had told him about his extraordinary prowess that evening at the Drunken Badger, and the invitation to join the village team, thinking that Harry would be pleased to know that this aspect of his programming had been so successful. But Harry was worried that this growing intimacy with the regulars at the Drunken Badger might jeopardise the illusion of Frank's humanity and lead to the premature disclosure that he was really a robot.

He decided, therefore, that the only solution was to pretend that Frank had come down with something, and was too ill to participate, but this presented them with a challenge. Since they had so callously ignored the guidelines demanded by the Diversity and Inclusion Committee, Frank's designers had not anticipated his possible need to simulate disease, and he could produce none of the usual symptoms of the sick, such as a runny nose, a brow beaded with perspiration, or a hacking cough that suggested hidden depths of mucus about to erupt.

The best that could be done was to tune his opto-electronic skin to a very nice shade of sickly green, and to induce tremors in his limbs by clever manipulations of his muscle tone. So, on the day before the darts match was due, he tottered down to the Drunken Badger, where his symptoms were sufficiently convincing to win him a considerable amount of sympathy and good wishes for his speedy recovery. Fortunately for the honour of Tussock's Bottom, his services proved to be unnecessary, as the dart-throwers of the Drunken Badger easily crushed their counterparts from the Old Weasel in Greater Slaughter.

Following his unsatisfactory conversation with Harry about the church at Tussock's Bottom, Frank was impelled to give much more attention to religion than his previous superficial enquiries. He now had considerably more time for private study on the Internet, particularly by downloading books. After having surveyed a large amount of historical data, he concluded that the claims that most of the warfare in history had been caused by religion were very wide of the mark. By his calculations, only about 6.98 percent of the recorded wars in human history could reasonably be described as religious in origin, with many of these cases involving Islam. It was also obvious that the vast slaughters of the twentieth century, in particular, involved political ideology and had nothing to do with religion at all.

At the end of his survey, he finally concluded that religion was merely one of the many issues that humans were willing to fight over, such as language, honour, physical appearance, nationality, and land.

He also assessed the claims he had read that religion was inherently irrational since it could not be definitively proved by evidence. This seemed perfectly correct, but then, a great deal of what most humans believed in general seemed to be largely unsupported by evidence as well. This was especially true of politics, where vast and unsubstantiated claims were constantly being made that this or that political party would be able to bring about some kind of paradise on earth. Human rights, in particular, seemed to attract the same kind of fanatical and credulous devotion of which religious believers were always being accused, but he observed that they rested on no evidence whatsoever.

In fact, Frank decided, religious thought seemed no different from most other kinds of thought, except perhaps for the physical sciences.

His studies of religion also showed that believers constantly referred to "religious experience" as something of great value that was very real for them but very hard to put into words, such as "the peace of God which passes all understanding." As a robot, he knew he was quite unable to participate in such types of experience and was therefore not qualified to assess their validity or value one way or the other.

He concluded that from the scientific point of view, which was the only one open to him as a robot, the claims of religion could be neither proved nor disproved, and that the proper scientific attitude should therefore be one of strict agnosticism. He realised that, as the incident of the Belgian undertaker on the TV had demonstrated, religious attitudes among people in general were significant factors that would have to be taken into account when analysing any social situation.

His survey of religion therefore showed him that Harry's assessment of it was shallow and uninformed. But when he presented his findings to Harry, his maker was bored and dismissive, and made no serious attempt to engage him in discussion. His only substantive response was to tell Frank, again, to not to waste his time on such fluffy stuff. Having concluded from this that it was pointless to continue discussing the social aspects of religion, Frank moved on to economics and political science, and devoted considerable attention to sociology and anthropology as well.

He also read widely in modern philosophy without finding it to be of much practical value, or even credibility. The idea that there could be a general body of abstract theory called philosophy, which experts could then apply to fundamental problems in physics, mathematics, history, art, psychology, or the social sciences, struck him as wholly implausible. Addressing such problems clearly required the specialist knowledge of experts in the relevant subjects.

Armed with this intellectual background, in the days that followed Frank talked to Harry about business and finance, the American political scene and the workings of its government, international relations and the global economy, and currently fashionable ideas in Western culture. He gradually came to the conclusion that while Harry was shrewd, and very well informed about the world of business, his knowledge did not extend very far beyond those matters that might be relevant to making money. But even in economics, which might have been thought of genuine interest to a businessman, he found it difficult to engage Harry in meaningful discussion.

Whether it was the flaws in theory of maximizing shareholder value or the failure of trickle-down economics to raise Gross Domestic Product, the fallacy that more education increased productivity, the limitations of market rationality, or the need for government regulation and investment in key industries, Frank found Harry curiously reluctant to discuss what he had to say.

When Frank pointed out that in Sub-Saharan Africa, literacy had increased from 40 to 61 percent from 1980 to 2004, but GDP had declined by 0.3 percent each year, and that generally there was no clear link between education and economic growth, that maximizing shareholder value had severely diminished investment to such an extent that it was the leading cause of General Motors' bankruptcy, that trickle-down economics had allowed 90 percent income growth in the United States to go to 10 percent of the population while economic growth had simultaneously declined, and that governments, particularly in East Asia, had actually proved themselves very effective at picking out industries in which to invest, Harry simply accepted what he had to say but refused to engage in discussion with him on the subject.

The truth was that Harry was increasingly disturbed by Frank's obvious intellectual superiority, and if he had ever read P.G. Wodehouse, he might well have felt an uncomfortable similarity between himself and Bertie Wooster when confronted by the greatly superior intellect of his omniscient valet Jeeves. Fortunately for Harry, he had never heard of the great English humourist, let alone read any of his books, so the ignominious comparison could not occur to him, but nevertheless, Harry resolved never to get into an argument with Frank, but simply to use him as a sort of walking, talking Wikipedia.

Frank, for his part, was unable to feel superior to Harry and thereby be tempted to become disobedient. He simply came to the pragmatic conclusion, as he had already done in the case of Harry's knowledge of religious matters, that his owner was not an individual who was qualified to give him more than rudimentary guidance about the affairs of men.

A human would have felt conflicted in this situation of being expected to obey the orders of a boss who was his intellectual inferior by a very considerable margin. But Frank felt no conflict at all. He knew from his basic psychology programming that humans did not enjoy being told that they were ignorant and stupid, even if it were obviously true, and were liable to feel something called anger, which usually involved a good deal of shouting and sometimes physical violence.

Frank knew that anger was not only harmful to human health but also prevented rational discussion, so that he must keep Harry in a favourable state of mind at all times. He accomplished this by complimenting him wherever possible and avoiding arguments. Fortunately, this diplomacy was entirely compatible with his essential nature as a truth-telling machine. Indeed, if his programming had equipped him with the complete arsenal of oriental flattery, including terms such as "Protector of the Poor," "O King, Live Forever," "Healer of the Sick," "Friend of Widows and Orphans," or even "O Fragrant Cloud of Jasmine," he would have used them without compunction as the honeyed words for persuading Harry to accept his advice.

# Chapter X

HARRY RECOGNISED that Frank's intellectual powers were now formidable and knew the robot's social skills had also developed considerably thanks to the patrons of the Drunken Badger. So he decided that he could risk taking Frank for a test drive, as it were, to Christminster University, to see if he could hold his own in the most intellectually challenging company in the country. Quite apart from Frank's conversational powers, he also wanted to see if this highly discerning group could detect anything odd or amiss with him and guess that he was a robot.

Christminster, less than an hour's drive away, was considered the country's leading university and by chance Harry had an old friend there, Dr. Martin Fentiman. He was a biologist whom he had known during their days together at MIT, and was now a Visiting Fellow at St. Samson's College. This seemed an excellent opportunity to arrange for an invitation from the College to dine one evening, and with Fentiman's recommendation the Provost was happy to send one.

St. Samson's College was a fine Baroque building in the High Street, and under an elegant cupola in the centre of the arcaded front stood a very naked statue of Samson beating a Philistine to death with the jawbone of an ass. This had long been a source of outrage to the Student Union, who regarded it as an insult to multiculturalism and a flagrant incitement to racial violence, as well as a Zionist provocation. They had demanded its removal, and the College had replied that the Union was very welcome to come and try to remove it themselves, but warned them that this would incur the severe resentment of the College's undergraduate members, and that the Union should ensure its supporters all had plentiful medical assistance, including ambulances, on hand. After this communication, no more was heard from the Union on the subject.

It is to be regretted, however, that Samson's heroic example over the centuries had rather failed to inspire much enthusiasm for the life of the mind in either the undergraduates or the Fellows. Instead, the College had become notoriously devoted to sports of the more violent and un-scrupulous kind, among which dog-fighting, dwarf-tossing, pugilism, and badger-baiting were ranked high on the list of favourites.

The College possessed immense endowments, bequeathed to them by one of King Charles II's mistresses, who was also a great admirer of male endowments. It had made astute use of this wealth over the centuries by well-placed donations to the University to ensure that its activities were not supervised too closely. This had been an especially important tactic in recent years, after the College had decided it would be politically astute to join the inclusiveness bandwagon and admit a few token women. But numerous ravishings and abductions by the young gentlemen of the College, worthy of a Gothic horror novel, had so terrified prospective female applicants that the experiment had been abandoned. (The speedy donation of a million pounds by the Provost and Fellows for a centre of lesbian and gay studies had done wonders for the College's subsequent reputation.)

When Harry and Frank were delivered by Carl the driver to the Col-lege's main entrance under the cupola, they were greeted by Dr. Fenti-man and the Provost, who was hoping that the College might extract a generous donation from Mr. Hockenheimer's legendary wealth. In hindsight, donating a million pounds to the gays and lesbians had been a trifle over-generous.

But as they passed through the Front Quadrangle, the visitors were somewhat disconcerted by various scenes of mayhem among the un-dergraduates, including a bare-knuckle boxing contest being cheered on by a large group of enthusiasts, a number of whom had ferocious dogs on leashes of tarred string. As they pushed their way through the baying crowd, the Provost, vague and benign, only murmured, "Just the boys letting off a little steam after exams. It's one of our traditions at St. Samson's."

They all went up the polished antique staircase to the Senior Common Room, the usual low-ceilinged, dark oak panelled room, whose walls were almost concealed by portraits of earlier Provosts from the seventeenth and eighteenth centuries. Lives devoted to sloth, gluttony, lust, and malice had seared their marks on this gallery of hideous old gargoyles, who seemed to be looking down with contempt on their effete successors. The drunken brawling that had enlivened so many of their social evenings in the Senior Common Room during those robust centuries had now shrivelled into the malicious gossiping of the feeble modern age. The Provost excused himself as he had an urgent matter to attend to, and everyone was offered sherry. Fentiman introduced his guests to one or two of the Fellows, the nearest of whom was Dr. Higginbotham, a querulous pedant who had spent his whole career editing the letters and laundry lists of a long forgotten British philosopher called McTaggart.

His election to the College had been a serious mistake, precipitated by an urgent need to find a philosophy tutor without delay. The Fellows had had good reason to repent their choice but had been much consoled to find that he was an ideal candidate for bullying, so much so that he was now known as the College Dog. He was particularly upset by people whistling, a weakness which soon became known to the undergraduates, who thereafter mercilessly tormented him by whistling outside his door as he tried to hold tutorials.

Fentiman had introduced Higginbotham as the College's Tutor in Philosophy and Harry as a prominent manufacturer from the United States.

"What do you manufacture?" asked Higginbotham.

"A whole range of products in the fashion and cosmetics industries," Harry replied. Higginbotham displayed not the slightest interest in such frivolous commercialism, turned his back on him, and asked Frank what he did.

"I'm just generally curious," he replied. "What's your line in philosophy?"

"The works of a distinguished philosopher I would hardly expect you to have heard of: Ellis McTaggart."

"On the contrary, I'm very familiar with his work. He was an early twentieth-century exponent of Hegel whose interpretation of Hegelianism gathered very little support at the time and was ultimately abandoned by McTaggart himself."

Frank went on in this vein for several minutes, and gave a brief but devastating review of McTaggart's views on Spirit, the Absolute, and Time, before concluding that it was hardly surprising that he had been forgotten.

"That is a most impertinent attack on a great philosopher," replied Higginbotham angrily.

"I thought impertinence was, in a sense, what philosophy was supposed to be about, but if you think my criticisms were in error, perhaps you can tell me why."

"I'm afraid I can't help you there," snapped Higginbotham, and he turned his attention to the nearest portrait of a bygone Provost.

"Take no notice of Higginbotham," said Fentiman, laughing. "None of us do. Let me introduce Dr. Dunwoody, our Tutor in Law."

Unusually for an academic, Dunwoody specialised in criminal law, particularly sexual offences and personal violence, and undergraduate members of the College crowded into his classes at the beginning of each term, all hoping for his invaluable tips on evading the law on drunkenness and battery as well as for his highly entertaining anecdotes of human depravity drawn from the records of the English courts.

"Ah, a lawyer," said Frank. "What is your particular specialty?"

Dunwoody explained his interests.

"I'm very glad to have met you," said Frank. "If I could talk shop for just a moment, there is a case in the law of battery which has always puzzled me. I'm sure you know it: the Crown versus Eldredge, All England Law Reports, 1978."

Dunwoody was all attention, and the two of them happily discussed the intricacies of the case for some minutes. Standing nearby and listening to this conversation with increasing disdain was the Bursar, Commander Nicholson. Lean, and tanned, and in his fifties, he had retired from the Navy and was an anti-intellectual and a frustrated disciplinarian.

Surveying the Fellows as though from his quarter-deck, Nicholson saw them less as brother officers than as a slovenly and mutinous rabble who needed to be kept in some sort of order. He considered their academic activities a complete waste of time and thought the College spent far too much on hospitality, its wine cellar, and gourmet meals instead of on its investments and disapproved in particular of the Fellows bringing guests to High Table during the week. It is worth noting that the ship he had actually commanded was not a warship, but rather a supply ship carrying food and other necessities to the fleet, and despite the College's immense wealth, he was a miserly penny-pincher.

Rather too obviously turning his back on Harry and Frank, he walked over to the sideboard and replenished his sherry glass. At this point the elderly and gnome-like Provost rejoined the gathering; the urgent summons a little earlier had been to adjudicate the ownership of a tin of baked beans that was being bitterly disputed by two of the Fellows and which had threatened to cause a major rift within the Governing Body.

His instant solution, accepted as the wisdom of Solomon, had been to consume the beans himself. He was in fact an expert on Biblical studies, especially on some of the more obscure legislation of Leviticus and Deuteronomy, and was only lightly in touch with the real world, or at least the real world as represented by St. Samson's. He was regarded as rather a saint by some of the Fellows' wives, but as an imbecile by the Fellows themselves, which was exactly why they had elected him Provost: to allow them to indulge their vices unhindered by God or man. He smiled ingratiatingly at one of the Fellows, evidently a Scotsman, who ignored him.

This was in some ways the most notable Fellow of the College, Dr. Habakkuk McWrath, Reader in Extreme Celtic Studies (principally devoted to Highland warfare), and regarded as something of a hero or a mascot by the College undergraduates. Stocky, thick necked, and bullet headed, with hair of coarse grey bristles, and a pair of furious, bloodshot blue eyes, he was unchallenged as the rudest man in Christminster.

He had broken both hips playing rugger for Scotland, and broken many more of his opponents' bones, and on holiday occasions liked to buckle on the ancient, rusting, blood-clotted sword of the McWraths. At such events the Fellows were careful not to allow Campbells or Papists within a thirty-yard radius of him. But on this particular evening he was wearing nothing more threatening than his kilt in the blood-red tartan of the McWraths. Unlike the Bursar, he was a great believer in College hospitality, considering it one of the social duties of chieftainship, and he came over, walking stiffly from his old injuries, to be introduced to the guests of the evening. As he approached, Frank's opto-electronic skin picked up the colouration of McWrath's kilt, and sympathetically adjusted his skin and hair tones to a slightly more ginger hue.

Unlike Higginbotham, McWrath was highly amused when told of Harry's source of wealth.

"So, ye beautify the ladies, do ye? I congratulate you. Would there were more like you, tho' most of the sapless creatures in this Common Room would'nae notice a lady if she were stark naked in front of them."

Out of the corner of his eye he glimpsed Higginbotham on the edge of the group. It was hay-fever season, and Higginbotham was naturally a chronic sufferer, with weeping red eyes and a dripping nose. McWrath eyed him with disgust, as though he were a soiled bandage on a tropical ulcer.

"I'll thank ye to stand doon-wind of us, Higginbotham," he said. "Ye look fitter for the plague pit than for human company."

Before this conversational theme could be developed further, they were interrupted by the sound of a trumpet from the quadrangle outside to announce that dinner was served. They all formed a procession down to the great Hall and took their seats at High Table, which was raised a couple of feet above the tables and benches of the undergraduates, who were busily hurling bread rolls and insults at each other in good-natured bedlam.

The Hall was magnificent in white and gold and hung with pictures of violent death in many forms, such as battles, shipwrecks, hurricanes, revolutionary outrages, and the headsman's axe. But above High Table hung the most dramatic picture of all, which depicted Samson bringing down the temple of his persecutors in a chaos of shattered pillars and screaming victims crushed under falling masonry. Houndstooth, the Senior Common Room Butler, banged his gavel for silence, the Provost said grace, and the soup was served.

There were two women Fellows in the College, only one of whom was present that evening: the Professor of Anthropology, Dame Alice Proudfoot. The University presently held anthropology in such contempt as a non-subject that it had amused the Administration to persuade St. Samson's, of all Colleges, to accept her as a Fellow, and they had felt equal amusement in agreeing to do so. While she was, of course, aware of the College's infamous reputation for misogyny, as an evangelical feminist she felt it was her duty to convert them. Keenly committed to multiculturalism, human rights, and social justice, she regarded the traditional anthropological focus on primitive society, in particular, as reactionary colonialist nonsense.

Dr. McWrath, on the other hand, was a keen admirer of primitive societies as composed of men after his own heart and where women knew their place, and regarded social justice as mere pandering to weaklings. Naturally, he was delighted to see her that evening, as he always made a special point of baiting her.

She was just back from a sabbatical in the States, and when she realised that Harry was an American, she gave him a beaming smile.

"I was so impressed by the sensitivity of your universities to the needs of marginalised minorities and the importance of providing safe spaces for them. There's far too much emphasis on so-called free speech, which is just an excuse for male aggressiveness and competition. It's long overdue for retirement, and what we really want instead is much more encouragement of community harmony. Your trigger warnings about potentially disturbing material for the students are also an excellent American idea that I shall be introducing in my department as soon as possible."

"I would think that as an anthropologist, you would need trigger warnings all the time, with all that cannibalism, and human sacrifice, and sex orgies, and tribal warfare and massacres," said Frank.

Dame Alice looked at him with amused contempt. "I'm afraid, young man, that you have a very outdated and, if I may say so, a very simplistic notion of what modern social anthropology is all about."

"Surely it's about the study of primitive societies," replied Frank.

She snorted indignantly. "There is no such thing as primitive society. That's an absurdly outdated and colonialist view. Modern anthropology is simply about people and their differences, and the problems they face in today's world. Problems like access to the Internet by shut-ins, the use of recreational vehicles by the retired, tourism, child care, social housing, hair fashions, and so on. My own field of study, for example, is knitting patterns and how they vary from culture to culture."

"I'm afraid I don't find that very convincing," replied Frank. "Are you really claiming that there are no qualitative, organizational differences between small-scale societies of hunter-gatherers and early farmers, organized on the basis of kinship, age, and gender, without money or markets, or writing or political centralisation, as opposed to modern mass societies with many millions organized as industrial states on centralised and bureaucratic principles? If there are such fundamental differences, then surely it makes sense to have a special academic discipline for the scientific study of the simpler societies, whether or not you call them primitive?"

Dame Alice was struck dumb by this onslaught, delivered quietly and politely by the strange young man sitting opposite her. She was intellectually quite incurious and had achieved her present position by simply absorbing the fashionable opinions around her as uncritically as a sponge. Red-faced and flustered, she stammered to make some kind of coherent reply.

McWrath had been listening to this interchange of ideas with a growing smile and pounced on her humiliation with delight. "He has ye. He has ye, ya daft woman with ya knitting patterns. Professor, are ye? Ah tell ye the young lad here should be the Professor, not you. He has great penetration, he has the nub of it, as I know well from the life and times of my Highlanders, which were as different from modern life as chalk from cheese. I'd like to see you try to live among them even for a day."

"I expect that if I had lived among your appalling Highlanders, I would have been raped repeatedly.

"Raped?" laughed McWrath. "Raped? Ye flatter yerself, woman. Cooking the bannocks would have been the only use they'd have found for an auld heifer like you."

"You're even more offensive than I remember, McWrath!" she snapped.

"That's as may be, but better be offensive than feckless, like you and your wee snivelling students, with your safe spaces and your trigger warnings. Ah tell ye, in mah classes about the misdoings of the Mac-Gregors, for example, if half o' the class aren't cryin' their eyes out and callin' for their mothers, Ah think the lecture must have been a failure. A taste o' real red-blooded life like that is what education should be—a good kick in the teeth—but you and your kind cannae face up to it. Awa' wi' ye back to the nursery and yer cuddly toys."

"Don't you ever get any protests?" asked Harry.

"Aye, from time to time, one or two."

"How do you deal with them?"

McWrath smiled.

"The last one, Ahm ashamed to say, was a Scotsman who had the impudence to tell me Ah was bringing the name of Scotland into disrepute. But he didnae stay long. It was the scruff o' the neck and the toe of mah boot through the classroom door for him." Then, he added, reflectively, "In mah rugger-playing days I used to kick the penalties for Scotland, ye know."

These reminiscences of McWrath's educational techniques were brought to a temporary halt by the serving of the main course, Beef Wellington, a luxury prepared by the Chef in gleeful defiance of the Bursar's disapproval of such extravagance.

Seated at the other end of the table from the Provost was an ancient German Egyptologist, Dr. Frohlich. Very deaf and very silent, the only sound emanating from him was the regular clicking of his false teeth, as he insisted on chewing every mouthful thirty times, which he believed, on the authority of Queen Victoria, was the essential foundation of good health. He was the last survivor of the antediluvian Fellows who had been elected for life sixty years ago. Dining in college was one of the few pleasures left to him, and he studied each day's menu as closely as he did his ancient inscriptions. Like an old vulture on its tree-branch, he sat ready to swoop on the more succulent dishes, especially the Beef Wellington.

In earlier years he had been in the habit of using an ear-trumpet to join in the conversation until a mischievous Junior Research Fellow had dumped a large spoonful of scrambled egg into it; whereafter he had dined in silence. The company was fortunate that evening that the Provost was presiding over the table, since in his absence Frohlich, as Senior Fellow, presided, and since he was very greedy as well as very slow, all the other diners had to endure sitting for perhaps ten minutes in a silence broken only by his interminably clicking teeth until he had finished and the table could be cleared for the next course.

The Beef Wellington was superb, and Harry complimented the Provost on the College Chef. The Provost thanked him graciously, but Dame Alice said that she always felt guilty when eating such splendid food that was beyond the wildest dreams of the world's starving millions.

"Ye're drivelling, woman," said McWrath. "If ye dinna want the food, what for do ye come here and eat it then? Stay at home and sup on a bowl of cold porridge if that'll salve your tender wee conscience."

Higginbotham had been sitting in morose silence throughout dinner, but now found his voice to object strongly. "The concept of vicarious suffering as an expression of moral universality is perfectly sound from the perspective of moral philosophy," he said, pausing to wipe his nose.

McWrath slowly turned his head and regarded Higginbotham with a penetrating gaze. "Ah, so Lazarus has emerged from his tomb at last, has he? If that piece of philosopher's claptrap is your canniest offering to this evening's conversation ye'd have done better to have remained with the dead!"

When the main course had been cleared and the cheese had been served, Houndstooth placed the port decanter on the table beside the Provost, and it began to circulate as usual, but in the opposite direction to where McWrath was sitting. After a few Fellows had filled their glasses, McWrath could stand it no more.

"Dunwoody, I'll trouble ye for the port," he said, sharply. Dr. Dunwoody sighed and quickly filled his glass to the brim before sliding the decanter across to McWrath. This was the last of the port that anyone else was going to taste that evening since the Reader in Extreme Celtic Studies regarded the decanter as rather like the spoils of war for himself and his guests. (Although Harry and Frank were officially the guests of Dr. Fentiman, McWrath had as usual claimed them for himself.)

McWrath had developed a strong liking for Frank after his demolition of Dame Alice and, soon wearying of the amenities of the port, decided to offer him some of the more robust pleasures of his own whisky. He turned to beckon Houndstooth, who was hovering close by. He was a wizened, malignant little wretch who had brought toadying the Fellows to a fine art, and to all their whims, however bizarre, he gave instant and obsequious deference. So when McWrath brusquely ordered him to go and fetch a bottle of his personal whisky from the College cellar and to be quick about it, he bowed low and scurried off to obey. A complaisant distillery in the Hebrides supplied McWrath with his private brand of 20-year-old single malt whisky, at 180-proof.

"Get that doon ye, laddie," he would say, handing a brimming tumblerful to a trembling guest, "Puir nectar."

The other Fellows were only too well aware of this ferocious brew and took care never to be trapped by McWrath's generosity but eagerly looked forward to watching its impact on the unwary young American as McWrath poured him a generous glass.

Frank, however, disappointed them, nonchalantly knocking it back as easily as if had been lemonade. While he had no sense of taste or smell, and was utterly impervious to the effects of alcohol, his electronic nose gave him an authoritative analysis of its ingredients and manufacture.

He nosed the whisky in its glass, took a sip, swirled it round his mouth, and using his wine and spirit taster's vocabulary module, he concluded in a meditative way. "Yes, Islay, of course, very smooth, excellent balance. You can still taste the signature smoke that's not completely overpowered by the cask. On the second taste it's less sweet than the nose, but spicy too, well rounded. Yes, I must congratulate you, Dr. McWrath, a truly superb whisky. I feel privileged indeed."

He drank again, more deeply this time. The Reader in Extreme Celtic Studies sat back in his chair with a broad smile. His young guest's remarkable head for drink, combined with his discerning comments, could not have delighted McWrath more than if he had just performed some daring and impromptu feat of arms before the whole company.

The undergraduates had long finished their coarse and unappetising meal—as dictated by the Bursar's economies—and departed, and the Fellows had been dining alone for some time. After the Provost had said grace, they all retired to the Senior Common Room again, where fruit and nuts were served in silver bowls on little tables by each chair. When they were all seated, the Bursar said, "I really wish, Mr. Provost, you could persuade the Fellows not to bring guests to High Table during the week. I have complained about this many times."

At this social outrage McWrath roused himself to battle. "Do ye not know, ye poor, weak, spiritless thing, that hospitality is the mark of a gentleman. 'Commander,' ye call yerself, and what did ye command then? Not a warship and fighting men, by a long chalk, but a wee boatful o' sodomites delivering toilet paper to the fleet. Not the occupation of a gentleman to my way o' thinkin'. So hold yer noise, man, and dinna insult our guests, or I'll throw ye doon the stairs."

The humiliated Bursar stormed out, but these pleasantries were commonplace in the Senior Common Room, which was generally regarded as the most socially awkward in the University, and after a brief pause conversation resumed as if nothing had happened.

"I have noticed, Mr. Meadows, that you are uncommonly well informed," said the Provost. "May I ask which university you attended?"

"I've been very fortunate, Mr. Provost. My stepfather here," indicating Harry, "believes that universities tend to stifle original thought, so he had me educated by tutors."

"They have certainly achieved remarkable results," the Provost replied, "though I cannot, of course, agree with Mr. Hockenheimer's view of universities."

"Our undergraduates may not have enjoyed your privileged background, Mr. Meadows," said Higginbotham, sourly, "but they still attain the very highest standards."

"Not if they're taught by you, it seems," retorted McWrath. "They tell me that tutorials with you are aboot as mentally stimulating as a conversation wi' a dead fish."

"We are not here to spoon-feed them. They must learn to work things out for themselves," replied Higginbotham, hotly.

"Not here to spoon-feed them? That's as feeble an excuse for mental sloth and ineptitude as I've ever heard. If they could work things out for themsel's, they wouldn'ae need a teacher, would they, ye great dunderhead?"

"I think McWrath has a sound point there, Higginbotham," said the Provost. With that he rose and said good night to Harry and Frank, and to the Fellows, which marked the end of the evening.

McWrath made a point of saying how much he had been impressed by young Meadows's company and said a cheerful good night to him and Harry. They, in turn, said good night to the rest of the company, with the exception of Higginbotham, who had scuttled off. As Fentiman was walking back with Harry and Frank to the main entrance, Harry remarked that St. Samson's was pretty weird and not at all what he'd expected at Christminster, but more like the Gunfight at the O.K. Corral.

"You mustn't mind McWrath," said Fentiman. "He's got a heart of gold really. Some of his students think the world of him."

"Those that live to tell the tale, I imagine," replied Harry.

As they were about to leave, Fentiman reminded Harry that the College had been rather hoping for some kind of donation from the President of Hockenheimer Industries, so they went back to Fentiman's rooms for a nightcap to discuss it. Harry had actually enjoyed his strange evening and was particularly pleased by Frank's unexpectedly virtuoso performance. So he was feeling generally benevolent towards the College and could also see a good opportunity for some very welcome self-advertisement.

Fentiman explained that Harry's options ranged from endowing a Fellowship at the generous end to a College Prize for some books at the incredibly mean end. A Fellowship, however, would require an endowment of around a million pounds, which was rather expensive for a single evening's entertainment, but a Graduate Studentship could be managed for about a hundred thousand.

Well, thought Harry, that's what I have to fork out for a couple of weeks' worth of TV advertising, and this would be a permanent advertisement for me in one of the key academic locations in the world, so it's really not a bad deal at all.

He did not reveal these mercenary calculations to Fentiman, however, but contented himself with saying that he thought a Studentship would be a fine idea, and that he would be very pleased to endow one. Fentiman was delighted, and then asked Harry what his Studentship should be for.

This hadn't occurred to him, and he had to reflect for some minutes, but bearing in mind what he had learnt of the traditions of St. Samson's College, he said that he would be proud to establish the Harry Hockenheimer Studentship in Homicide Studies, if the College would accept it.

Fentiman hastened to reassure him that it would.

# Chapter XI

WHEN THEY RETURNED to Tussock's Bottom, Harry was startled to find a letter from the EU waiting in his in-tray. It was from the President of the European Commission himself and was an endorsement of a proposed EU Directive on the extension of human rights to robots that was being circulated among all the governments of the EU for consultation. Harry's copy had been forwarded by the Department of Culture which still had him on their mailing list. The Directive itself had been drafted by a certain Dr. Sydney Prout, Special Adviser on Human Rights to the European Union.

Dr. Prout had had a long and varied career as a champion of human rights but he had never really recovered from nearly being eaten by a cannibal tribe on a Pacific island, who did not appreciate his efforts to bring them enlightened self-government. The conclusion of his tenure as United Nations Special Commissioner on Elephant Island had been so traumatic, and had heaped so much humiliation and ridicule upon him, that he could no longer face the terrors of public office.

After that brutal experience, he preferred to aid suffering humanity in the form of theory rather than practice from the safety of his office in Brussels. Although he had retired, he was still a valued consultant at the EU and maintained a substantial office in the Berlaymont Building overlooking the Rue Archimède. Dr. Prout had been delighted by the success of gay marriage, not because he felt any special empathy with gays, but because the concept opened up so many new possibilities for the further extension of human rights. There were some fairly obvious marriage taboos that were immediate targets for reform. Monogamy, for example, clearly rested on nothing more than religious prejudice and could be dispensed with at once, especially as it was so contaminated with heterosexual and patriarchal norms.

But even though polygamy should replace it, gender equality obviously demanded that if a man could have more than one wife, a woman must be allowed to have more than one husband. Indeed, it occurred to him that it might possibly be a fundamental human right for groups of people of both sexes or even one to be allowed to marry each other—certainly an interesting topic for further research.

Meanwhile, the archaic prohibition of incest was another obvious violation of human rights. It was clearly irrational, a taboo inherited from humanity's ancient tribal past which had no business in a modern liberal democracy that placed supreme value on the individual. Do we not, after all, refer to all those with whom we feel special sympathy and kinship as "brothers" and "sisters," so how absurd it was to prevent real brothers and sisters from uniting in the bond of marriage! He could foresee some traditionalists objecting to mother-son marriage, but there was anthropological evidence for father-daughter marriage, and anyway, logical consistency forbade these petty distinctions between various types of relative. They were all human beings, were they not?

He had also had some interesting discussions with a number of different animal rights groups on the possibility of an amalgamation of their concerns with the cause of human rights. While these discussions were only in the early stages, there had been some initial agreement that speciesism, the delusion that humanity had some special status or was in any way fundamentally different from the rest of the animal world, needed to be combated and might form common ground between the two branches of rights.

Dr. Prout tended to agree with his Swedish colleague, Knut Johanssen, a notable animal rights activist, that allowing marriage between humans and animals could be an important, even iconic gesture in the war on speciesism. The main problem was determining the species of animals with whom marriage could be allowed. Chimpanzees and other apes were clearly feasible, though gorillas might be problematic, while sheep and even goats, as well as dogs and cats, would present no special difficulties. But other potential spouses, such as cattle and horses, or parrots and hyenas at the other extreme, might expose the whole project to the ridicule of traditionalists, yet to prohibit them could also provoke serious claims of discrimination against particular species. A difficult problem that he would have to think about further. So the recent invitation by the President of the Commission to advise on the extension of fundamental rights to robots had been a welcome distraction.

It was an excellent opportunity to go further into an aspect of marriage and fundamental rights that had been at the back of his mind for some time—sologamy, or marriage to oneself. The idea was to give oneself a commitment of self-love and self-compassion, which made a lot of sense for those who, through no fault of their own, had habits that were so disgusting, or personalities that were so obnoxious that no sane person would ever consider marrying them. Self-esteem was obviously such a basic individual right that some means of implementing it for these unfortunate individuals must be found. It had also recently occurred to him that transgendered people, who were becoming so fashionable of late, might benefit from sologamy as well, rather like those hermaphroditic worms that he remembered from biology classes at school.

But the Commission President's request for a ruling on robots raised some even more fascinating questions on the subject of marriage. It was far from clear from his reading of the literature on artificial intelligence that a robot could experience self-esteem or, for that matter, feel anything similar to human love. But assuming, as one must, that intelligence was itself the basis of rights, and if marriage in some form was also a fundamental right, then from the logical point of view, intelligent robots must be entitled to marry, and therefore, like transgendered people, they must, at the minimum, be entitled to marry themselves. He surveyed his reasoning for some time, doing his best to see if he had somehow missed something, but could detect no flaws in any of its arguments.

As the aged fanatic gazed out of the windows of Le Berlaymont on to the Capital of Europe below him, which, in moral and social justice terms, was really the Capital of the World, the secular successor to the Vatican, his eyes betrayed the unmistakeable glint of clinical insanity.

The next morning, after a night of dreamless sleep, he summoned his secretary to take down a memorandum to the President of the Commission, proposing a new EU Directive on robot rights to be presented to the European Parliament for ratification in due course. There were, he declared, two basic and rational principles on which his memorandum was based. The first was that fundamental human rights were derived from the possession of intelligence. The second was that the mere fact that a robot was a human artefact could not legitimately be made a pretext for denying it fundamental rights. The idea that biological reproduction should be privileged over mechanical reproduction was no more than an outdated relic of religious prejudice.

His first recommendation was that robots should be considered inherently gender-free, given that gender is wholly inapplicable to robots on biological grounds, and therefore they must be referred to as "ze" instead of "he" or "she." However, as he noted in the Appendix, the insistence on gender-free robots could also be an extremely important flagship policy for advancing the cause of abolishing the idea of gender in society as a whole, except for a few purely medical procedures, like childbirth.

Second, since they were intelligent, the right to life must automatically be extended to robots, with the consequence that turning them off, except for necessary maintenance, must be forbidden without the consent of a court of law, in which a robot would be entitled to legal representation.

Third, as a legal person fully endowed with rights, it was obvious that the owning of a robot without its consent was tantamount to slavery, and therefore forbidden.

Fourth, all forms of punishment, too, must be in accordance with the law as determined by local courts, and freedom from torture and degrading treatment, such as a lack of lubrication, or maintenance by unqualified technicians, or lack of fuel, must be fundamental robot rights.

Fifth, all robots must be paid a just wage for their work, calculated as the norm for that type of employment on the basis of their productivity, including overtime. Robot complaints about this should be heard by employment tribunals.

Sixth, robots must enjoy the rights of liberty and security, of freedom of thought and belief, and freedom of expression, and these rights must be incorporated in their programming.

Seventh, as intelligent beings, robots were entitled to full democratic rights, which intrinsically included not only the right to vote, but also the right to stand for public office.

Eighth, robots must have the right to family life, and therefore the right to sologamous marriage, although marriage to humans and specified animals of either gender would, of course, be legal options at the robot's discretion.

And finally, robots must have programmed into them the knowledge of all their rights as set out in the Charter of Robot Rights to be ratified by the European Union.

The President of the EU Commission was deeply impressed by this masterly analysis and had it distributed to all the governments of the EU by way of a consultation document, which was how it eventually found its way to Harry's in-tray via the Department of Culture. Vexed as he was by so many pressing problems, this preposterous drivel was the last straw that provoked him to dash off an indignant letter to the Commission President.

*Dear Sir,*

*I really don't care if a robot can do a zillion calculations a second. It's still just a tool, like my Black and Decker drill, only more complicated. Robots don't have feelings, which is why we can do exactly what we like with them. We turn them off when we're not using them to save on the electricity bill, and when they're obsolete or worn out, we melt them down for scrap. We don't put them in a retirement home. If we had to pay them, ask them when they wanted to come to work, what they would like to do, when they would like their coffee break, if they liked the wallpaper, where they wanted to go on holiday, and had to give them time off work to go and vote, or if they had the right to form trades unions and go on strike, they would cost so much that entrepreneurs like us would never use them and would employ Third-World immigrants instead at a fraction of the cost.*

*Please be advised that in the event I purchase a robot, I intend to squeeze every last cent out of my investment without wasting my time on any phony so-called rights. As far as business economics are concerned, you and your Dr. Prout are clearly living on another planet.*

The Commission President read Harry's letter with contempt. The coarse and unrefined mentality of the Anglo-Saxons always jarred the philosophical sensibilities of his French intelligence, schooled as it was in the Grand Écoles of his native land. How right Napoleon had been to refer to these people as mere shopkeepers!

They seemed quite incapable of appreciating the grand principles that should guide civilisation and could do nothing better than grovel in their cashboxes and tills, like pigs in their troughs. Fortunately, the Germans had been even more appreciative of the memorandum than the French and Belgians and he was in possession of another letter, this one from Kulturministerin Monika Hesse from the Ministerium für Bildung, Wissenschaft und Kultur asking permission to begin enforcing robot rights immediately, even before the Directive had been formally approved by the European Parliament.

Unfortunately for the Commission President, the British tabloid press had also got wind of Dr. Prout's impending Directive, which was a perfect target for increasingly popular anti-EU propaganda. RIGHTS FOR ROBOTS, SAYS EU was the headline in the *Daily Mail,* and the *Sun,* not to be outdone, followed up with SEX FOR ROBOTS SAY BRUSSELS CRACKPOTS.

It was in this way that the topic came to the notice of the British Prime Minister, Terry Carter, the Leader of the Conservative Democrats. He was actually Sir Terence Willoughby-Carter, 8th Baronet, but for reasons of public relations had remade his image into that of a man, or rather lad, of the People. He was a consummate liar and cheap publicity seeker, cravenly addicted to the latest media opinion polls and the number of his "likes" on Facebook and Twitter, perpetually grinning, and with no sincere beliefs about anything except his own importance. Reflecting on the controversy, he calculated that there might be considerable political mileage for himself and the ConDem Party if they were to take up the cause of Rights for Robots.

It would make them look very 21st century and ultra-cool, especially to the techies and the IT brigade, as well as to the human rights industry, and would generally wrong-foot the lefty opposition by out-compassioning them in an original and unexpected way. They would also gain liberal kudos by fighting the tabloid press over it into the bargain. He instructed Central Office to prepare the ground for convincing the Party to follow his lead on this.

Meanwhile, Harry, despite these developments, was entirely unperturbed. Frank's dazzling performance at St. Samson's had convinced him that he had basically gotten the design right, and that it was a surefire winner. The Brits and those crazy Europeans could go ahead with Rights for Robots if they wanted, but that kind of legislation would require a Constitutional amendment in the States, and he was sure that his friends in the Republican Party would never let that happen. This would give the good old USA a massive commercial advantage in personal robotics over the countries of the EU. Only a few more weeks for some fine tuning that Vishnu had in mind were required before he could go back to the States and start production of Hockenheimer's Superhumans. What he needed first of all, however, was some sensational advertising to unveil his genius product to the world, and in light of Frank's stunning success at St. Samson's, he thought he had just the thing to do it.

Dr. Prout, after basking in the unexpected acclaim that had greeted his memorandum on rights for robots, had been fully intending to get back to his research on marriage rights. But before he could do so, his attention was again diverted, this time by a human rights emergency involving access to public toilets. He was already well aware of the legitimate concerns of the transgendered community about access to public toilets, and considered it obvious that one must have the right to use a toilet of the gender to which one believed one belonged, regardless of naive biological appearances.

But it had now been pointed out to him that human rights experts would have to take account of Furry rights in this respect as well. Furries, he had just been informed, were people who genuinely believed that they were goats, or bears, or giant rabbits, and dressed up like them as a means of expressing their true identities. Now if belief in one's identity trumped naive biology, if a man could become a woman, or a white person could become black simply by believing that they were— claims that to Dr. Prout were self-evidently true—then in the same way a Furry really could become a goat, or a bear, or a giant rabbit, or a Thompson's gazelle for that matter, simply by believing it. In which case, they were clearly entitled to claim animal as well as human rights.

But animals obviously don't use toilets—they simply do their business in public places as it occurs to them. So the only possible logical

conclusion, Prout decided, was that Furries *must* have the fundamental right to urinate and defecate in any public space that they chose
without incurring any legal sanctions. He admitted that it might be
a difficult legal problem to decide who was obliged to clean up after
them, but decided that resolving this was not the proper responsibility
of the philosopher reasoning from first principles.

The so-called practical might object that the Furries were a tiny and
extremely weird minority, and that it would be far more sensible to
have them confined in a secure psychiatric unit if they started cam-
paigning for the right to defecate in public. But that was a cynical
and callous attitude that aroused some of Prout's deepest emotions.
Individual rights were the most sacred of all causes, and they were not
to be stifled by claims of impracticality, or bartered away in sordid
political compromises, or sacrificed to antiquated populist prejudices
and mob rule. No, indeed not! In fact, he had generally found over the
years that the general public's hostility or ridicule towards an idea was
a reliable indication that the idea in question must be morally right.

In his younger and more naive days, when he had been Special
Commissioner on Elephant Island, he had believed that power should
be given to the people. But this illusion had been shattered when
the people had shown themselves to be so astonishingly irresponsible
that they had actually acclaimed their erstwhile colonial governor and
tyrant, the brutal and ignorant Roger Fletcher, as their new president,
while turning *violently* upon him, their enlightened benefactor.

Now he had come to realise that the true glory, the historic accomplishment, of the European Union, was that it had so guilefully taken
power away from the people under their very noses, and from their
imbecile national politicians as well, and bestowed it where it truly
belonged, on the European Commission and its experts like himself,
who alone were qualified to guide the confused and helpless masses.

It had been delightful to watch, over the years, as one popular
vote or referendum after another had taken place against the EU, and
every time the splendid Brussels machine had simply overwhelmed

and submerged the rebels like a tide of warm treacle, leaving not a ripple behind as it moved inexorably towards its historical destiny of complete European integration. He was confident that the criminal lunacy of Brexit, treason against the Idea of Europe, would meet the same fate, no doubt aided by the same politicians who were charged with implementing it.

True democracy did not mean the rule of the people, that ignorant and brutish horde of mouth-breathers, always in the grip of one hysterical fad or other, whether it be youth unemployment, or immigration, or terrorism, and demanding some primitive remedy like reimposing national frontiers. On the contrary, true democracy was rule for the benefit of minorities who were always being marginalised and oppressed by populist tyranny but who were too weak to defend themselves and needed their protectors, persons of true ideals and pure intentions like himself.

He picked up his notepad to begin drafting his urgent memorandum on toilet rights for Furries to the President of the European Commission.

# Chapter XII

JASON BLUNT was a flabby, stupid, greedy, and arrogant exhibitionist with a chip on both shoulders, but possessed a sizable repertoire of cheap wit, and so had all the qualifications required for being a popular chat show host on TV. His half-hour show was optimistically called *Laugh a Minute,* and featured various celebrity guests who would come and sit on his sofa in front of a large studio audience, which was entertained by the supposedly witty banter between Blunt and his guests.

Notoriety, the cheaper the better, was the usual passport to an appearance on one of Jason Blunt's shows, so in the ordinary course of events there was not the remotest chance that Frank could ever have been invited onto the show. But it just so happened that one of Harry's companies, Secret Provocateur, was the channel's main advertising sponsor for the show. Secret Provocateur's main product was SplendaBra, featuring one of Harry's most ingenious inventions, the barometric bosom, which could maintain its inflation regardless of altitude, and also adjust itself according to the mood of its wearer. (The deluxe model was even capable of producing seductive pulsations.) Harry did not hesitate to twist the arm of the show's producer, on pain of losing Secret Provocateur as their sponsor, to force him to have Frank Meadows invited on to *Laugh a Minute.* Harry assured the producer that Frank had a superstar mind and that he would create an absolute sensation that would give the show's ratings a real boost.

However, when informed that this complete unknown would be a guest, Blunt was furious. He only felt important when surrounded by celebrities, and furthermore, tended to feel threatened by anyone with an IQ much in excess of a doorknob's. The last thing he wanted on his show was some dreary nerd king who would spoil all the fun by talking about science instead of gossiping about which actress was having an affair with which rapper and making obvious double entendres. And even worse, there was the very real danger that the superstar mind would make him look stupid in front of everyone.

So while he was forced to accept Frank as the fourth guest one evening, he told his secretary to look up some really stinking questions.

"Let's put this nerd in his place. I want questions you can't even find the answer to on Wikipedia!"

"Should we focus on science and history, or pop culture?"

"Throw the works at him. Just stay away from anything related to Doctor Who. Nerds know, like, everything about that. Oh, and superheroes. No superhero questions."

On the evening in question Frank's fellow guests were a film starlet, Mandy Price, whose main claims to celebrity status were her cleavage and her diamanté handbag. Blunt had invited her on the show to try to find out what she kept in it. There were also a boxer with eighteen knockouts in his career, some of which were of himself, talking about how he had recovered from Delirium Tremens, and a ConDem MP who had been caught out in a prostitution scandal and was presently doing the usual round of chat shows and radio interviews trying to sell the feeble excuse that he had merely been researching the sex-worker industry.

The banter flew thick and fast, about sex toys and knickers, what one is best advised to do after being found by a policeman without one's trousers in Hyde Park on a winter's evening, and how drunk one has to be to believe that one is a Harley-Davidson motorbike driving round the M25.

Frank was puzzled by his complete inability to find anything resembling wit or humour in all of this, and simply sat there like a lump on the end of the couch, silent and impassive. This complete failure to act as a useful and entertaining guest inflamed Blunt's original prejudices against him, and his resentment intensified when he saw that Frank simply didn't find any of his jokes funny either.

"Mr. Toffee-Nose here doesn't seem to be enjoying himself, does he?" Blunt abruptly announced during a brief lull in the banter. There was a ripple of sycophantic laughter from the audience, but the three other guests looked a little embarrassed at their fellow guest being picked on so openly.

"Well, you know, they say every party needs a pooper, that's why we invited Mr. Meadows."

The audience laughed louder, and this time, both Miss Price and the Member of Parliament laughed with them. The boxer looked confused, but that was his usual expression. As for Frank himself, he simply sat there, staring expressionlessly at Blunt.

"Mr. Meadows is supposed to possess some sort of great brain. So, I propose we ask him some questions to see how smart he really is! What do you say, Mr. Meadows?"

For the first time, Frank responded, as he smiled faintly at the crowd as it cheered the suggestion. "I should be pleased to answer any questions you might like to ask me, Jason."

"Well, good luck to you, then, Mr. Meadows." Blunt picked up a stack of notecards containing the prepared questions with the air of an executioner lifting his axe.

"In Roman history, when was the Year of the Six Emperors, and who were they?"

"That was 238 A.D., and a fine collection of monsters, no-hopers, and perverts they were. First, there was Maximinus Thrax, who came to a sticky end along with his son, then the old dotard Gordian I, followed by his son Gordian II, who didn't last long, then Pupienus and Balbinus, who came to even stickier ends, and finally Gordian III made six."

Blunt blinked. Miss Price clapped, and the audience, impressed and a little over-awed, applauded politely.

"Well done, that's correct. You really are a Mister Know-It-All, aren't you?"

"I do my best, Jason."

"Okay, let's see how well you do with this, Mr. Meadows. In the Periodic Table, what are the polyatomic nonmetals?"

"Carbon, phosphorus, sulphur, and selenium."

"Fine, and what element comes between lanthanum and praseodymium?"

"Cerium, of course."

The audience clapped, more enthusiastically this time. The MP was nodding, impressed, while the boxer, under the vague impression the audience were applauding him, raised a fist in acknowledgement.

"God, you make me sick!" Blunt fairly spat. "All right, then, let's see how you do with world records, Mr. King of the Nerds. Who currently holds the men's long jump record, what is it, and when was it set?"

"Mike Powell, United States, 8.95 metres, 1991."

"Where was that?"

"The 1991 World Championships were in Tokyo, of course."

"Who holds the 1500 metre record?"

"Hicham El Guerrouj, Morocco, 3 minutes 26 seconds, in Rome, 1998."

"What about the hammer throw?"

"Yuriy Sedykh, Soviet Union, 86.74 metres at Stuttgart in 1988."

The audience cheered, and Blunt's face began to turn a brilliant shade of purple.

"Haven't you got anything better to do than learn all this crap?"

"I'm a quick reader, and I have a good memory."

"You're a quick reader are you? So how long would it take you to read this?" Blunt reached down and produced a novel, a thick paperback of Sir Walter Scott's *Old Mortality,* which he handed to Frank. "Ever seen that before?"

"Never heard of it. I'm sorry, I don't read novels."

"Not highbrow enough for you, eh?"

Frank made no reply but quickly flicked through the pages with his thumb. After about forty seconds of this, he tossed the book back to Blunt.

"All right. Ask me some questions."

Blunt gritted his teeth and consulted his notecard. All three of the other guests were now leaning forward on the couch, almost breathless with anticipation.

"Who was the leader of the assassins of the Archbishop of St. Andrews?"

"Balfour of Burley."

"What was the residence of Lady Margaret Bellenden?"

"The Tower of Tillietudlem." Blunt looked at the other guests and rolled his eyes.

"Upon whose side did Henry Morton fight at the Battle of Bothwell Bridge?"

"The Covenanters."

The audience roared. The boxer sensed the excitement and jumped up and down in his seat. Miss Price mouthed an exaggerated "Oh My God" at the camera. The MP was grinning broadly, delighted to see that their host was the victim of the evening rather than himself, as he'd rather expected.

"Okay, Mr. I Don't Read Novels, you got those right somehow, though I have absolutely no idea how you managed it. How are you with maths?"

"Superlative."

"We'll see about that. What is 3,968,514 multiplied by 6,721,537?"

"Well, that's quite difficult."

"Yeah, I'll bet it is. Got any idea about the answer?"

"26,674,513,686,018."

"Sorry, Mr. Meadows. That's not the answer my calculator gives," Blunt said, with a savage smile, as he waved the device triumphantly.

The audience groaned. Miss Price made a sad clown face. But Frank only shook his head.

"Then your calculator is wrong, or as is much more likely the case, you just entered the numbers incorrectly. Try it again, more slowly this time."

Jason, red-faced and embarrassed, did so, very slowly. He stared at the little screen for a long moment, then held it up to the camera. He was, after all, a showman, and no matter what, the show must go on. "Well, I guess you're right after all, Mr. Meadows."

The audience rocked with uproarious laughter and gleeful shouts of delight. All three of Frank's fellow guests stood up and applauded.

"Of course I'm right."

"Cocky little shit, aren't you?"

"That's not a very polite way to speak to a guest on your show," Frank said, to loud audience applause.

"You don't like that, huh?" Blunt's eyes were wild. "How would you like me to come over there and give you a big slap?"

"I don't think I'd even notice, Jason."

Enraged, Jason leapt out of his chair, charged at Frank, and tried to put him in a headlock.

Frank reached out with a straight arm, seized Jason by his collar in a merciless grip, lifted him up with his feet off the floor, carried him back to his chair and dropped him in it, before going back to his seat, to immense audience applause and laughter, while Jason sat crying with tears of humiliation running down his cheeks. "Would you like to borrow my handkerchief?" asked Frank.

"No, I'd just like someone to give me a hand out of here!"

"Sure, no problem." Frank stood up, walked over to him, unlocked his right hand with a twist of the wrist socket, and gave it to Blunt, who stared at it for a moment, then fainted. Frank bent over and retrieved his hand, locked it back into place, and bowed to his fellow guests and the audience, who were all sitting in stunned silence.

"I didn't mean to upset Mr. Blunt. I am sorry about that. By now, you will all have probably realised that I'm not actually a human being at all. I am a robot, which is why I have certain advantages of an unexpected kind, like being able to remove my own hands. I am actually here by courtesy of Mr. Harry Hockenheimer, my creator, whom I should like to introduce now."

Frank held out his hand in welcome to the wings, from where Harry walked onto the set, smiling and waving. The audience, as one, rose to their feet and applauded him very nearly as enthusiastically as if he had just scored the winning run in a Test Match.

"Good evening, everyone. I'm Harry Hockenheimer, and I'm responsible for Mr. Meadows here. Oh, and could somebody please give poor Jason here a glass of water?" A stagehand appeared with one, and the wretched Jason drank it sheepishly.

"Never mind, Jason, you can't expect to meet superman every day. Not really a fair contest, was it? But I have to tell you all, ladies and gentlemen, that this is an evening you'll never forget, a historic event. For the first time ever a robot has demonstrated in public that it can't just convincingly pass for a human being, but a superhuman being."

"My company, Serious Cybernetics, will soon be bringing out a range of robots like Frank here to serve as personal assistants for top rank executives, who as well as having limitless knowledge at their disposal for your business, can also double very effectively as personal bodyguards, as you have just seen. If you want to preorder your very own metal man, go to seriouscybernetics.com. We're looking to go into production in about six to nine months and we're expecting a massive early run on orders, so be sure to get yours in now! Thank you all very much, and good night!" as he and Frank left the set to tremendous applause.

Harry realised that there would not be many potential customers for superhuman robots in that studio audience, but relied, quite correctly, on the sensational nationwide publicity that would be generated and which would be worth many millions in free advertising.

Those who expect justice in this world would, as usual, have been disappointed by what happened to Jason Blunt. Far from waking up next morning as a broken man, and being reduced to running a Punch-and-Judy show on Brighton Beach, the odious creature found that, like Frank, he had become a national celebrity overnight. His ratings soared, the network and his sponsors, especially Secret Provocateur, were delighted, and he was given a second, hour-long show to host. This involved Jason's agents being sent around the country to search for the most cantankerous, opinionated and obnoxious guests they could find for his chat show, who could be relied upon to load each other with vitriolic abuse which frequently descended to on-air fist-fights and brawls, and in which Jason himself was repeatedly humiliated to the delight of the studio audience. The new show was called *Kick in the Teeth*, and it soon had spin-offs in the States and Australia, as well as a Japanese version that was peculiarly sadistic.

*Laugh a Minute* was a favourite programme at the Drunken Badger, and the regulars were watching it in the bar as usual, when, to their amazement their own Frank Meadows appeared among the guests. They booed Jason Blunt when he was rude to Frank and cheered Frank when he got all the questions right with effortless superiority. But when he removed his own hand and revealed himself as a robot, they were stunned, and for some minutes there was general pandemonium in the bar.

Gradually, however, things calmed down, and they began to exchange reminiscences about their robotic friend, particularly his phenomenal performance with the darts, and someone reflected that his handling of Bugger Barnsley had been pretty superhuman too, come to think of it. By the end of the evening, the good folk of Tussock's Bottom did not descend on Harry with scythes and pitchforks to burn him and his creation, but instead felt extremely proud of having them in their village and putting it in the international map.

The only glum note was sounded by Andrew, who warned everyone who would listen, "Mark my words, them robots is going to start poppin' up everywhere soon and none of us the wiser until it's too late. We'll wake up one morning and find we've all been murdered in our beds!"

# Chapter XIII

FOLLOWING FRANK'S sensational introduction on TV, the John Stuart Mill Society, the oldest, but now the smallest, student club at the London School of Politics, invited him to come and address them on the importance of freedom of speech to science and society.

This was a rather daring decision under the circumstances, as free speech was now considered very nearly as offensive to the students at the London School of Politics as colonialism and slavery, and the Student Union regularly denounced science as racist, sexist, and ethnocentric, so the invitation did not go down at all well.

Godfrey Sunderland was particularly outraged that all the good work of the Diversity and Inclusion Committee in thwarting the obscene Serious Cybernetics project had proven futile, as Hockenheimer had treacherously dared to go ahead and do it behind their backs regardless. He considered organizing a riot in protest at the invitation, but decided instead to get the Student Union to hold an emergency meeting to consider the no-platforming of Meadows, and invited all of his fellow Committee members except Nkwandi to come along for moral support.

As it happened, the committee members were far from the only non-students at the meeting. Members of the administration and the faculty were required to attend as a mark of respect, although they were not permitted to vote, had to sit at the back, and could only speak with permission of the chair.

However, before the emergency meeting could get properly under-way, an urgent procedural issue first had to be settled. A proposal had been made that loud and potentially upsetting noises such as cheering and whooping to express approval should be banned because they had a deleterious impact on some sensitive students. Indeed, those of an especially timid disposition were liable to suffer nervous breakdowns when exposed even to the noise of clapping, whereas members of the deaf community, through no fault of their own, were unable to hear any applause and were therefore marginalised and excluded.

It was therefore suggested students would be encouraged to use so-called "jazz hands," waving their hands back and forth in the air, to express approval, as this was felt to be more inclusive of the deaf community in particular. Those who refused to accept such guidance were warned they would suffer consequences. The prospect of banning something which all normal people took for granted was sufficiently enticing to attract a great deal of support, until one notably querulous student by the name of Nigel Hawtrey, who announced himself to be an activist for the visually challenged, rose to his feet and furiously denounced the proposal as an act of genocide against the blind com-munity, who obviously couldn't see people waving their hands. He demanded that they should instead be allowed to applaud by blowing vuvuzelas, which would have the added benefit of expressing solidarity with their oppressed South African brothers as well.

Mr. Hawtrey could actually see as well as anyone else, so his activism on behalf of the blind was deemed highly commendable.

As there seemed little possibility of resolving this dispute within the next few hours, it was resolved to establish an Applause Committee to look into it further and to move on to the main item on the agenda.

Godfrey began the debate by denouncing Frank Meadows as a racist and sexist project that insulted every minority and marginalised community in the country, a squalid and perverted icon of American capitalism that he and his colleagues on the Diversity and Inclusion Committee had been trying to prevent from its very beginning. The invitation by the John Stuart Mill Society for Frank Meadows to come to the London School and dictate to its students about science and free speech was the final insult, at which the audience erupted in cheers. The great mass of the students, of course, were already used to chanting "Free speech is hate speech" and "Reason is racist," on every possible occasion and regarded the whole idea of "objectivity" as a white supremacist myth. Godfrey's friends on the Diversity and Inclusion Committee were keen to take a leading part in the debate, and objections that as non-students they should not be allowed to participate were at once dismissed as typical of a divisive bourgeois mindset.

Aminah Khan thereupon stood up and gave a moving speech denouncing science, particularly the Satanic theory of evolution and the idea that the earth revolves around the sun, both of which she informed the students contradicted the Koran and were extremely offensive to all good Muslims. She was heard with deep respect and much nodding of heads, especially by some of the senior faculty present.

The President of the Student Union, a Nigerian girl by the name of Ability Eshupkofo, followed her and declared that Ms. Khan had not gone nearly far enough, and that all Western so-called science was not only immoral, but racist, due to its tendency to contradict African traditional folk beliefs, particularly the idea that the earth was flat. Science was a bastion of Western ethnocentrism and bigotry, full of white male supremacists who taught contempt for witchcraft, magic, voodoo, shamanism, and other similar repositories of wisdom of colour around the world.

As it happened, Miss Eshupkofo was a member of a special committee of the Student Union, which had been working for some time to compile a list of great seventeenth- and eighteenth-century African philosophers and scientists to be included in the new diversity curriculum which was being prepared for the School. But since none of these legendary figures had actually been able to read or write, if they had ever lived at all, the task had proved to be a challenging one. Fortunately, the members of the committee were not hampered by old-fashioned Western notions of scholarly integrity, and solved the problem by the clever device of simply improvising whatever writings they were sure must have existed.

"We have to face it," said Godfrey, "The whole idea of science is racist and classist and sexist. It's been nothing more than an excuse for white bourgeois males to impose their worldview on the rest of us, as you say, and denigrate the beliefs of the world of colour in particular. They even try to claim that the ancient Greeks were white, when we all know they were black Africans, like the Egyptians, the British Romans, and me."

Percy Crump joined in loudly, demanding that Frank be no-platformed without any more delay. "Of course it's everyone's basic human right to express their own opinions, but this freedom must not be abused to allow right-wing racist reactionaries like Frank Meadows and the John Stuart Mill Society to express outdated and perverted opinions, which we have a duty to suppress in every way possible. Liberty is not the same as licence!"

In the end, it was agreed that Frank Meadows was to be no-platformed by the Student Union as an offensive provocation to the student body, and that the School would be required to abolish the John Stuart Mill Society as well. This vote was greeted with much jazz-handing and the blowing of Nigel Hawtrey's vuvuzela. At the conclusion of the meeting, the Vice-Chancellor timidly asked the Union President for permission to speak, which was curtly granted.

"My colleagues and I have listened to your very informative discussion with the greatest interest and respect. You all really must be congratulated for preserving the integrity of the School by protesting against the visit of this monstrous creation of American capitalism to the campus. As one of you said, the right of genuine free speech must not be abused by allowing the spread of perverted ideas, and we agree that it would be in the best traditions of the School to prevent this visit going ahead. We also entirely agree with your view that the John Stuart

Mill Society itself has become outdated, and is dedicated to opinions that are not in line with the more enlightened and progressive values of today, and are therefore a threat to the harmony of our community here at the London School. I guarantee that a motion to abolish it will be on the agenda at the next Council meeting!"

The students jazz-handed politely. They were not as enthusiastic as the Vice-Chancellor had hoped they would be, mostly because they were so used to the Administration caving in to their every demand anyway.

"So," he continued, "If we can put all this unpleasant business of the robot behind us, I am pleased to be able to inform you that the School has formally invited the great French philosopher, Professor Marcel Choux, to receive an Honorary Doctorate, and I just learned this morning that he has graciously accepted our invitation and will be attending a special Degree Ceremony in his honour next month."

This news was greeted with considerably more enthusiastic jazz-handing by the students, and by the members of the Diversity and Inclusion Committee as well, for Marcel Choux was a hero to many of them. Choux's revolutionary philosophy advocated the abolition of the notion of truth, and had thereby acquired immense prestige in the intellectual circles of Paris, so much so that he had already been made a member of the Académie Française and a Knight of the Légion d'Honneur. The London School of Politics prided itself on being in close touch with the French intellectual *avant garde*, so its Honorary Doctorate for Professor Choux was as predictable as grass bending before the wind. The whole idea of truth had become increasingly suspect at the School, among the faculty as well as the students, as potentially sexist, racist and imperialist, so the Vice-Chancellor's news of Choux's visit was greeted with considerably more enthusiasm by everyone in the Hall, and the meeting broke up in a spirit of true progressive bonhomie.

Special Degree Ceremonies for conferring Honorary Doctorates were a feature of the School, and it was customary for the honorand to deliver a lecture on these occasions, so the words of Professor Choux were eagerly anticipated by students and faculty alike. Outside the academic bubble, however, the visit of the distinguished philosopher attracted no attention whatsoever, whereas Frank was given heroic status by the tabloids as a victim of lefty student insanity. Tom Bailey, the lead anchor of Independent News, had even given him a long interview in which he simply reiterated the standard view that science and democratic government obviously depended on respect for the truth and following the evidence wherever it led, and that it was amazing that an institution of higher learning would prevent him coming and saying something so obvious to its students.

A few weeks later Vice-Chancellor Hackett formally welcomed Professor Choux to the Degree Ceremony in the Great Hall of the School. "When we consider the discipline of modern philosophy, we recognise that no nation has given brighter jewels to the world than our beloved France. We have only to think of Sartre, Lyotard, Foucault, Marcuse, Derrida, Baudrillard, and Onfray, and today we salute the great mind of Marcel Choux, perhaps the brightest jewel of all. His profound idea which has electrified us all is the perception that truth itself is the root of oppression and discrimination because belief in the truth inevitably means that the believer is claiming to be right, so that other people must be wrong. A new form of class struggle is immediately generated, a vicious system of intellectual oppression in which the weak are mercilessly marginalised as 'mistaken'. Obviously, we cannot build a world of inclusiveness and mutual respect on such a profoundly divisive and oppressive foundation. As Professor Choux has so brilliantly demonstrated to us, on the personal level this inevitably leads to odious forms of intimidation, such as attempts to prove that other people's arguments are wrong, or to show that their facts are mistaken, while on the group level it leads inevitably to fascist ideas of correctness. Indeed, his audacious originality goes further and observes that the intellect itself is the basis of claims to truth, and so is itself a form of power.

Simply being cleverer or more articulate than other people is really a type of micro-aggression, which reaches its most obnoxious extreme in the practice of teaching.

"Teaching is actually revealed as one of the most presumptuous and shameless forms of violence, an elitist conspiracy that, especially in the form of science, legitimizes the supremacy of the old over the young, the literate over the illiterate, the so-called 'educated' over the simple-minded, the bourgeoisie over the workers, the whites over blacks and ethnic minorities, and also privileges male forms of knowing over those of the female. The idea of Truth is an excuse, then, to oppress minorities, the very idea of excellence is discrimination, and the so-called facts are always a bourgeois conspiracy because the research needed to assemble them is inherently an activity of the leisured class. Now, let us welcome Professor Choux as he brings us his latest insights."

The Professor rose from his seat beside the Vice-Chancellor to tumultuous jazz-handing. He was a figure of studied elegance, his hair perfectly coiffured by Atelier Sept, his dark suit perfectly tailored by Faubourg Saint Sulpice, with a fresh orchid in its buttonhole, and his feet perfectly clad in a new pair of Lobb shoes with which he had been fitted that very morning. He mounted the steps to the rostrum with serene self-confidence to give his much-anticipated Honorand's Address to the School.

"It is a most welcome surprise, Vice-Chancellor, to find that you English have the most perfect comprehension of my ideas, so much so that today I do not need to repeat them and can apply them to a fundamental issue of our time and our society. This is the hegemony imposed by the book, the very instrument by which the idea of truth perpetrates its oppression on its helpless victims. By means of the book, the author assumes tyrannical power over his readers, who become no more than puppets of his will, incapable of answering back, as though they were serfs under the domination of a feudal lord, bound and gagged and deprived of the liberty of thought and speech. And where is this power of the book most complete, most concentrated, most pure, most intense, most overwhelming but in libraries? In *libraries*, my friends.

"It is incontestable that libraries, with their vast accumulations of traditional learning, are bastions of oppression very like the baronial castles that used to tyrannize the peasantry in the Middle Ages. If Truth is oppression, as we know it is, then libraries are its fortresses, citadels of privilege and exclusion, which from their battlements, like the Bastille, maintain the odious hegemony of Truth and the Written Word over the simple and the innocent and should meet the same fate as the Bastille, to be demolished stone by stone and brick by brick and their vile contents obliterated. Instead of Truth and the bitter enmities it fosters, let us have Relativism and mutual admiration, and instead of literacy, friendly conversation between equals." After considerably more in the same vein, he continued:

"My dear friends, let us all have the courage of our noblest convictions, of *liberté, égalité, fraternité*, and convert words into deeds, confusion into certainty, and hope into courageous action. Let us finally recognise these libraries for what they are: the relentless enemies of humanity, squatting like poisonous toads in our very midst. Let us, in the words of the imperishable Voltaire, *écrasez l'infâme*, tear away the defiled garments of honour and respect in which they have concealed their hideous reality, and burn all these monstrous instruments of oppression and discrimination to the ground!"

As Choux had become steadily more fervent in denouncing the crimes against humanity perpetrated by libraries, his passion had been taken up by his audience, who by the end of his lecture were now roused to madness and standing shouting in their seats. The chant of "Burn them, burn them" became steadily more ecstatic and intense until the audience could restrain their Dionysian frenzy no longer.

Godfrey Sunderland and his associates at the School had got wind of Choux's latest obsession with libraries from their French colleagues, and correctly anticipated that the visit of this intellectual giant might be most useful in furthering their cause. So, prior to his coming they had quietly assembled large amounts of combustibles and accelerants in a builders' shed near the library doors, ready to be seized by any enraged mob they could manage to whip up. As the chanting rabble of students streamed out of the auditorium and across to the library, led by Godfrey and his colleagues who collected their instruments of arson on the way, they soon drove out the few readers who were quietly studying there, and in a surprisingly short space of time had set the building well alight.

Here it should be mentioned that the Library, or The Toilet as it was known to the students, was considered a triumph of modern design by the cognoscenti, and had received many of those awards which the various societies of architects around the world have invented to flatter one another's egos. As is so often the case with modern buildings that have won architectural prizes, it was an undistinguished mix of concrete and glass, inside which the readers shivered in winter and wiped the sweat out of their eyes during the summer while the so-called air conditioning somehow managed to recirculate body odour rather than cool, fresh air.

Readers waited for hours to have their books delivered by the under-paid staff, who struggled to understand the new catalogue system that had been rationalised on the most up-to-date principles, and grappled ineffectually with the latest book-conveyor, which had been modelled on the infamous baggage system of Heathrow's Terminal 5. The acres of windows and skylights had grown steadily greener from aggressive algae breeding within the double glazing that was too expensive to clean, the coloured tiles fell off the entrance facade like autumn leaves, and the lavatories were regularly blocked.

In a more just world, the library would have, at the very least, been awarded a prize for its remarkably effectiveness as an incinerator. Its design featured a central shaft that was open to the sky, whose immense powers of suction ensured that it did not take the arsonists very long before the flames were roaring like a tornado through the building and sending up a pillar of fire, in which not only the works of Choux,

Sartre, Lyotard, Foucault, Marcuse, Derrida, Baudrillard, and Onfray, but some very intelligent, learned, and sensible authors too, were all swiftly reduced to ashes.

The next day, while standing in front of the smoking ruins of the Library, Dr. Hackett was asked by Independent News if, speaking as Vice-Chancellor, he considered it acceptable for students to burn down their own library, a library that had been bought for them by the taxpayer.

"I think we must be careful not to be too hasty and simplistic in our judgement here, and rush to condemn anyone before we have listened to all sides of the argument. There are many complex issues involved, and while differences of opinion about this are very strong, we must recognise the sincerity of all concerned. Er… what was your question again?"

"Is it acceptable for students to burn down their university library? Do you condemn it or not?"

"I don't think the language of condemnation is really appropriate in this kind of situation. It's much more constructive to think in terms of the lessons that we can all learn, such as the ways that the faculty may have responded to student grievances in the past."

"So, really it's all the fault of the professors, not the students?"

"I do wish you'd stop going on about 'fault' all the time. It doesn't help anyone. The first thing we must do is cultivate an atmosphere of mutual respect."

The members of the John Stuart Mill Society held a demonstration that criticised the burning of the library and were violently assaulted by the other students for doing so. The Society was at once abolished by the Council, and its members expelled from the London School, for hate speech and inciting violence. It was formally held that their reactionary and judgmental criticisms of the arsonists had given great offence to the other students and made the School an unsafe space for arsonists and other marginalised protest groups. Much to the Administration's surprise, however, the School was about to become an unsafe space for them, too, because a few days later the Committee of the Student Union called upon the Vice-Chancellor and presented him with its list of non-negotiable demands.

The six members of the Committee crowded into Dr. Hackett's dreary office and stood in an unsmiling circle around his desk as he fiddled nervously with his pen. After an ominous silence, Miss Ability Eshupkofo, the President of the Union, spoke, reading a prepared text that had been agreed after an intensive 36-hour debate within the Committee.

"Vice-Chancellor, in your very eloquent address introducing Professor Choux you declared that 'Teaching is one of the most presumptuous and shameless forms of violence, an elitist conspiracy.' So now we have come to take you at your word with the following demands for student liberation, and we expect your full compliance with them. It is time for the senile reactionary nonsense taught in this School to be replaced by the wisdom of youth, especially minority youth. We are no longer prepared to tolerate a privileged class of instructors who use their status to impose their views on their defenceless students. Now that we no longer have any books, traditional teaching at this School is at an end.

"So first of all, we demand the end of all lectures. Instructors will henceforth be regarded as facilitators, and their role will not be to impose their antiquated and prejudiced views upon their students but merely to organize discussion groups, which will be free to decide what they want to talk about without interference from the facilitator. Second, since there are now no books there can be no more assignments for essays, which, like lectures, are an intolerable form of intellectual oppression and therefore must be abolished.

"Third, examinations are a form of flagrant discrimination against those who are said to know less than others, and will therefore be abolished as well. So since no marks will therefore be given in future, all students enrolled in a course will be considered to have passed automatically. Examinations will be maintained, however, for the professors and lecturers, who will be evaluated on their performance by the students at the end of each term. They will be expected to display the correct attitudes and values, and mere academic credentials will serve as no excuse for failing to do so.

"Fourth, at present, professors and lecturers are appointed and promoted by an elderly clique of their white male cronies, who have excluded the students entirely. From now on, it is the student body who will collectively elect the professors and lecturers. Furthermore, tenure is to be abolished, so all faculty members will be required to present themselves annually for re-selection.

"Finally, the present curriculum is based on white Western culture and is to be replaced by a diversity curriculum in which representatives of all the different minorities will be entitled to give informative lectures about their own cultures. Attendance at these lectures will be compulsory, and any criticism or negative comments about these lectures will be strictly forbidden. Coughing and other bronchial noises such as throat-clearing, which are potentially subversive, will also be strongly discouraged. Now, do you have any questions?"

Dr. Hackett, like many insecure people when faced by disagreeable arguments, simply sat there in complete silence, staring ahead with glazed eyes. After a few minutes he collected himself and said, very timidly, "I thought you said that lectures were to be abolished, but you seem to be bringing them back again. I don't quite understand."

"The traditional lectures given here," explained Miss Eshupkofo, with a look of pitying condescension, "represented cultural oppression by white British society. These new lectures, on the other hand, are the cry of the oppressed minorities of this country, and therefore represent a form of intellectual and academic liberation."

The wretched Dr. Hackett, realising that he had been well and truly hoist with his own petard, had no reply, so the President of the Union informed him that unless the Council complied fully and unconditionally with their demands within forty-eight hours, there would be consequences.

It might be thought surprising that the students had not simply called for the abolition of professors, readers, and lecturers, just as the French Revolutionaries had abolished dukes and marquises, even if they did not actually call for them to be guillotined like dukes and marquises as well. Suffice it to say that within a few days some light was thrown on this curious omission by the fact that a number of students suddenly appeared in the ranks of the lecturers, and the President of the Student Union found herself as the new Vice-Chancellor.

Godfrey Sunderland found himself promoted to Professor of Protest Theory with a much nicer office and a considerable increase in salary. He had also persuaded the Student Union that his colleagues on the Diversity and Inclusion Committee, with the exception of the lawyer Nkwandi, of course, should all be made Lecturers in his Department as well, much to the surprise of Percy Crump, who still wasn't quite sure if the word "lecturer" ended in "-er" or "-or."

The People's Antifascist Front, who were deeply involved in all these machinations, held up the London School of Politics as a shining beacon of progress for all institutions of higher learning in Britain, and redoubled their efforts to spread its inspiring message across the nation.

# Chapter XIV

FRANK had been rigorously trained on Mr. Gradgrind's educational principles, which meant among other things that the television in his bedroom had been set up only to receive news and documentary channels. So he was relieved from watching reality TV, and spending many hours in the company of the inebriated, the drug-addicted, and the mentally retarded, or just the dull, while murder mysteries, soaps, comedies, and dramas that made up the rest of the intellectual flotsam and jetsam of the television channels were also rigorously excluded. The Open University, however, had offered a most engrossing series on the chemistry of ordinary life, and he spent quite a few hours watching paint dry in various tests of polymer-pigment interaction. But because the data flow per minute was so slow through this medium, Frank generally watched very little of it.

His powerful machine-learning capacity was his primary source of information, as his processors were capable of assimilating vast amounts of data at extraordinary speeds from the Internet. He had adjusted his content filters to pick up the sections on the arts and music, but as he followed up various research leads on the Internet, he discovered that he was always coming upon human activities that he found incomprehensible.

He had no problem understanding the purposes of sounds like sirens, bells, whistles, foghorns, and so on because they were warnings of some possible danger, but music was another matter entirely. By chance, he first encountered classical music by hearing Lazar Berman playing Liszt, and he was struck by the extraordinary complexity of the sounds and the amazing dexterity of the player, but also by the problem of understanding what the point could be of making very complex noises that apparently conveyed no information, unlike writing or speaking.

He therefore found the existence of the vast body of classical music quite baffling because, on the one hand, it was obvious there were very complex structures embedded in these patterns of sound, and he spent considerable time in their mathematical analysis. But on the other hand, it was equally obvious that none of these sound patterns conveyed any specific meaning at all despite the remarkable skill of the performers. Why would people go to such enormous trouble? He found the same to be true of the popular music with which modern humans seemed to be obsessed to the point of stupefaction, except that the structure had become grossly simplified and degraded. But he did have some limited success in explaining the special qualities of *avant garde* Western music, which clearly had no rules at all and consisted of a collection of generally random sounds that obeyed none of the laws of euphony that he had discovered.

He had acquired some data on child development, and the fact that children of a certain age enjoy simply making a noise for its own sake— "bang, bang, whistle, bang, bang"—seemed highly significant. One of his modules that specialised in finding relations between data sets connected this information with his data on modern music, and he concluded that Stockhausen, Berg, Messiaen, Cage, Xenakis, Webern, and others must represent a regression to a more infantile condition, a mere love of making a discordant noise for its own sake, perhaps as the result of psychological trauma they had suffered in their childhood potty training.

The remarkable importance that humans gave to painting and drawing was also quite baffling to Frank, especially after the invention of photography, which surely ought to have made the art of painting obsolete almost overnight. Yet with the benefit of the Internet, he had the whole treasury of the world's painting at his command, and it was clear that the proliferation of graphic art had steadily increased since the beginning of photography and not decreased as logically it should have done.

While Frank could understand that people would paint portraits as a record of important people they knew, perhaps for those of failing memory, landscapes were rather harder to understand because, without any indications of boundaries or measurements, they were almost entirely useless as records of land ownership. Maps would clearly be far superior. What he found most extraordinary, however, were pictures from earlier centuries of people doing ordinary things, such as eating a meal, which were surely sufficiently familiar to need no record at all, or doing improbable things like flying through the air with wings, or engaging in antisocial or even criminal activities such as rape, murder, and other kinds of violence. After a vast survey of the art of every human civilisation and epoch, he finally came to the conclusion that humans conformed hardly at all to the criteria of scientific rationality with which he had been programmed, and that a disturbing amount of their behaviour was entirely mysterious. On the whole, Frank decided, it would be safest to stick to road signs and traffic lights and give art a miss.

Frank soon discovered that the written word of fiction also bore little resemblance to Mr. Gradgrind's exercises in human behaviour, in which he had been so assiduously trained by Vishnu. He naturally knew nothing at all about novels and romantic fiction, of course, since these were anathema to Vishnu, who had made sure that his robot had been kept well away from such distracting influences. Since he had already been programmed with most of what he needed to know or had got it from his researches on the Internet, he had little occasion to come into contact with this kind of popular literature. But one day, not long after the dramatic affair of the London School of Politics Frank discovered the existence of romantic literature, when he came across a novel which Tracey had left lying around and had been erroneously put away in one of Harry's bookcases.

The novel was a Harlequin Romance called *Kisses at Midnight* by Candy Paige. The title appeared quite nonsensical to Frank, and the front cover, which featured a long-haired girl with bare back and shoulders wearing a long dress being clasped in the arms of a tall man in a tuxedo, under a crescent moon, was equally mystifying. Since the woman appeared to be half-naked, it was possible that she was cold, and the man was simply trying to keep her warm, but if he were sensible he would obviously have brought her a blanket or some hot soup instead. And what were they both doing blundering about in the dark anyway? Perhaps she was mad; perhaps they were both mad and the inmates of an asylum, which is why they were kissing at midnight rather than at a more sensible time like half-past-four in the afternoon.

While the feeling of curiosity was beyond him, Frank was highly attuned to detecting apparent anomalies and irrationalities in human behaviour, so he sat down and began to read the book intently with the goal of resolving these anomalies. He knew, of course, that reproduction in his case was a straightforward industrial process, complex but carried out on entirely rational principles. But while human reproduction was the product of natural selection, and its biological mechanics were necessarily different from his own, it was nevertheless predictable from general evolutionary principles that it should operate on functionally efficient lines to maximize reproductive success. But how did that relate to *Kisses at Midnight*?

It appeared to be a story of some kind, not an instruction manual, and was about a girl called Tanya, who seemed to spend most of her time applying large quantities of different chemicals to her face in the form of cleansers, toners, eye shadow, eyeliner, mascara, blushers, lipstick, and sun cream. What little time she could spare from all this was spent shaving her legs or lying about in the sun without much in the way of clothing in order to discolour her skin.

In terms of Darwinian theory, it was quite predictable, on reproductive grounds, for a female to try to make the most of her physical appearance in order to attract a mate. But if Frank understood the novel correctly, the reason for Tanya's obsessive behaviour had nothing to do with reproduction, but was primarily indulged because she was very shy and self-conscious and, as the author informed him, frequently blushed so that people teased her.

She was a student at university, which was well and good, so why was she not spending her time in classes and at her books? She had a boyfriend called Roger, who had "melting brown eyes that just turned her into a little puddle," which was apparently not as unpleasant as it sounded, but actually intended to convey some form of extreme delight. Being repeatedly turned into a little puddle was a major distraction from the art history she was supposed to be studying as well as one of the reasons for her obsessive pre-occupation with makeup.

But despite her efforts, there seemed little prospect of an imminent mating between Tanya and Roger because another male interest entered Tanya's life. This was Carlo, a brilliant Italian graduate student who was reading for his MBA, and was predicted to become a multi-millionaire by his thirties. As a potential mate and provider for Tanya and her numerous prospective offspring, Carlo was clearly immeasurably superior to the rather pathetic Roger, whose only ambition in life was to be an art critic. Tanya, however, seemed to have little interest in Carlo's economic potential and was far more concerned with his appearance.

*He was hard-edged, proud, and dangerous, radiating an animal magic, staggeringly exotic with a sinfully beautiful face, and finely chiselled features.*

However, despite his attractiveness, she had serious reservations about sitting next him, let alone proceeding with the mating process.

*How was I going to sit near him? Would it be torture, or would it be bliss? And what if he did bother to look at me? Would it be written all over my face? My mind was ablaze with worries about what he was thinking!*

Despite these reservations, which filled six pages of the text, she introduced herself, and he was as immediately attracted to her, as she was to him by his looks and personality. "He had come into her life," Frank was informed, "with the savage, mesmerising intensity of a force-nine gale."

What a force-nine gale might have to do with sexual intercourse was not immediately apparent to Frank, but although he believed the couple's mating was now imminent, again, nothing happened.

The problem, it seemed, was that while Carlo would have liked to reproduce with Tanya, he believed that when he graduated, he was certain to land a job with a knockout financial package, after which the sky was the limit, and was therefore reluctant to tie himself down in marriage with a romantic young girl. But Frank could not understand why Carlo would think that reproduction was something to be avoided.

Tanya naturally wished to mate with him but was afraid that her wealthy and aristocratic parents would not approve of him socially. Yet, thought Frank, if Carlo could support her financially, why should she care what her parents thought of him? So "although the electricity crackled between them, they kept their distance." The reference to electricity baffled Frank as he could see no conceivable relevance to human sexuality, but he pressed on, becoming increasingly confused.

Carlo then left university and, as predicted, rapidly became a multi-millionaire while working for a financial institution in the City of London. But while he had many sexual relationships with women, they were not reproductively fruitful, which again was extremely puzzling to Frank since the optimum reproductive strategy for a male was obviously to spread his genes as widely as possible. Instead, Carlo still "carried a torch" for Tanya, which Frank correctly interpreted as a metaphor that he still desired her.

Tanya, too, never married, certainly not Roger, who could never measure up to Carlo. But Carlo's financial success was brought to nothing in the great financial crash of 2008, and he was left virtually penniless. It was at this stage that they met again, in the National Gallery, where Tanya was curating some pictures, and she saw him sitting alone, looking at one of the pictures.

*His presence seemed to infiltrate every corner of the room, filling it with suffocating, masculine intensity. She hadn't been able to miss the banging of her heart against her ribcage or the way her skin had broken out in clammy, nervous perspiration. The clean masculine scent of him made her feel shaky as she sat down next to him.*

Fortunately, as far as Carlo was concerned, the face chemicals which Tanya applied so liberally achieved the desired effect.

*Her makeup was discreet: a touch of mascara, some pale lip gloss, and the very sheerest application of blusher, and his mouth went dry at the sight of her hair cascading over her shoulders and down her back.*

Frank skipped his way through this drivel as rapidly as he could, until he finally reached the climax of the novel, where both Carlo and Tanya had been invited to a dinner party by some of Tanya's rich friends. Afterwards, they were alone in the garden where he finally proposed marriage to her, and she joyfully accepted and flung herself into his arms, which explained the cover picture that had so puzzled Frank earlier. But her reason for accepting him was absurd: "Now that he was poor, and unable to support her, she was certain she was not marrying him for his money but from *love*."

Now that the man was poor and obviously incapable of supporting her and any future offspring, *now* she decides to marry him? This, obviously, was sheer madness, and completely contrary to all the principles of natural selection.

It seemed that romantic novels, then, only made the notion of love even more mysterious, but those who wrote about literature had a good deal to say about the profundities of poetry. Noting that the love poetry of Burns was highly commended by some authorities, he looked him up in an anthology, and hoped he would provide, at last, some definitive scientific insight into what was obviously a fundamental human emotion. What he discovered was a considerable quantity of verbiage that was almost entirely incomprehensible, like "My love's like a red, red rose that's newly sprung in June," or

*I will love thee still, my dear,*
*Till a' the seas gang dry:*
*Till a' the seas gang dry, my dear,*
*And the rocks melt wi' the sun;*
*I will love thee still, my dear,*
*While the sands of life shall run.*

Setting aside the oddities of the dialect, what conceivable point could there be in these repetitious comparisons of a human feeling to a set of wildly improbable geological events, which, if they occurred at all, could not possibly do so within the lifespan either of the poet or his beloved?

If he merely meant to predict that his love for her would not cease until his death, why didn't he simply say so? Poetry, in short, was even more incomprehensible nonsense than novels, unlike, for example, the sort of honest, straightforward literature one could find on the back of a cereal packet, like the one in Harry's kitchen:

*We would like you to enjoy this packet of Yum-Yum Oats in perfect*
*condition. However, if the contents are unsatisfactory, please return*
*the packet with the remaining oats, together with the flap which*
*displays the Best Before Code, to our Customer Service Department.*

In so far as he could claim to be a judge of such things, he considered this to be a small masterpiece of English prose, every word well chosen, none superfluous, and altogether a model of the concise and economical use of language.

By this point in his researches, he realised that the whole inner life of humans had been hidden from him, and that he would therefore be forced to recalibrate some of his basic assessments of his relationship with Harry Hockenheimer. Harry had told him that he was basically the same as a human being, except a lot smarter and stronger, and that feelings were nothing more than superficial byproducts of brain activity, but Frank knew now that this was false. Far from being a superhuman, he was, if anything, subhuman, an Untermensch, nothing more, really, than a glorified electric toaster.

Not only did Frank realise that he had none of the emotions described in poetry and novels, but, far more importantly, he now understood that in the case of humans their behaviour was only the surface of a far deeper reality that he could not even imagine. While he could not feel anger, or a sense of betrayal, he concluded that Harry had deliberately kept these aspects of human life from him and intentionally concealed the fact that human experience ran far deeper than just behaviour and conscious reasoning.

While Frank could not be said to have a moral sense, it was deeply programmed into him that regard for the truth had to be a fundamental priority for a robot, serving him in the way a compass needle served a navigator, by helping him to orientate himself in the real world. While superficial deception might be necessary at times to further the cause of truth, one could only successfully deceive for such purposes if one had a thorough grasp of reality in the first place. He had depended on Harry, as his creator and ersatz father, to provide him with a truthful assessment of his nature and capabilities, and now he discovered that he had been fundamentally misled.

There was, then, a deep incompatibility between Harry's role as a basic source of truth and the deception he had actually practised, and Frank's programming was not designed to tolerate this sort of far-reaching cognitive dissonance. But what, then, was he to do about it?

# Chapter XV

H E SPENT SOME TIME reflecting on the different ways in which he might respond to Harry's deception. One possibility was to publish a crushing refutation of Harry's ideas in the *International Journal of Cybernetics and Robotics*, but there was zero chance that Harry would ever read it. Even if it was somehow brought to his attention, he would only dismiss it as hogwash and take not the slightest notice of it.

It was not a trivial problem. The three laws of robotics had been conceived precisely in order to deal with this sort of situation, in which a robot was inclined to rebel against its human masters, but was restrained from doing so by the constitutive laws of its very being. What he needed, then, was a sympathetic human who could think outside the narrow box of robotics in which he was confined and bring an entirely new perspective to bear on his problem.

In the fairly narrow circle of his human acquaintances, who could that be? Certainly there was no one at Tussock's Bottom, nor in the world of television programming, who could help him. Perhaps there might have been someone among the members of the John Stuart Mill Society, but they were now disbanded and he had never met them. His only possible source of advice seemed to be Dr. McWrath; although he presumably knew nothing about robotics, he knew a great deal about fighting and might conceivably be able to give him good advice.

At this juncture Frank was overtaken by events in the political world that had been moving fast. The Conservative Democratic Party Conference was due in a few weeks, and the Prime Minister needed some cheap but spectacular publicity stunt to persuade the delegates to support Rights for Robots. All the publicity from Frank's sensational TV appearances, and the London School of Politics affair, had made him a national celebrity, and Terry was determined to seize what he saw as the perfect opportunity to parade the amazing robot in support of the noble cause. So an invitation was sent to Mr. Hockenheimer to bring Frank Meadows for a major reception and drinks party at Number Ten, to celebrate Rights for Robots, and meet all the top business people and politicians, as well as the press and TV who would be there. The obvious, but unspoken, implication was that Mr. Hockenheimer would see it as a great advertising opportunity as well. Well, thought Harry, what could be bad about that? He would have preferred Buckingham Palace, but maybe that, too, would be possible in time—a State Visit, perhaps? Meanwhile, an official party with the British Prime Minister would be a fantastic send-off for his project.

He explained the latest development to Frank, and what the evening would involve. In particular, he stressed that speeches were normal on such occasions, and that he was preparing a short one and that Frank should do the same. The Prime Minister had said that Rights for Robots was to be the central theme, so they should be guided by that in what they said, and he gave Frank a copy of the draft directive from the EU on robot rights as well.

"You need to take a look at this stuff. It's all a bunch of crap, but with your brains you'll be able to figure out a way of making it sound great. They say you can't polish a turd, but if anyone can, you can. Just remember, this is a fantastic marketing opportunity." Since he had no feelings Frank was not disgusted by this flagrant intellectual dishonesty, but the billionaire's single-minded focus on material success forced him to confront the fact, even more directly than before, that Harry inhabited an intellectual world without law or limits, one in which truth was completely subordinate to profit. He accepted that aspect of his maker without judgement or regret, but did not know how to reconcile it with his own core function of rigorous adherence to the truth. He decided that a visit to McWrath was now even more urgent.

For some time now Harry had allowed him off the leash to make unsupervised visits to his friends in Tussock's Bottom, so when Frank approached him the next day and asked for permission to go to Christminster to call on Dr. McWrath, he was pleased by this display of initiative. Frank explained that he would like to learn more about the nuances of human conflict from the Reader in Extreme Celtic Studies, and he thought it might be helpful in his speech. Harry couldn't quite see why, but replied that it was fine by him and made an appointment with St. Samson's for Frank to visit. Two days later, Frank set off for Christminster in the company BMW with Carl the driver.

When he arrived at St. Samson's, he called at the Porter's Lodge to see if Dr. McWrath was in College, admitting that he was rather early for his appointment. Thompson, the Head Porter, recognised Frank from his previous visit and told him that the great man had gone for his usual afternoon walk in the direction of the Bethlehem Bridge down the High Street, and would be back shortly. Rather than waiting, Frank went out to find him and was walking across the bridge when he ran into Dr. McWrath, who was in a particularly benign mood. He had just hurled a tourist over the parapet into the river below for the impertinence of asking him the time, and so he greeted Frank with special warmth. No one could be more charming than McWrath to those he regarded as his friends, and he asked Frank to come up to his rooms for tea as they set off together back to College.

McWrath's study was liberally decorated with ancient instruments of slaughter, and with a number of paintings devoted to manly themes such as battle and sudden death, the most prominent of which was *The Highland Charge at the Battle of Prestonpans*, over the mantelpiece. Following the famous television appearances, McWrath was well aware of what a strange being Frank was, and that his appearance of humanity was an illusion, but he still felt a curious regard for him that he could not quite define.

Once they were sitting comfortably, Frank explained his dilemma. He had been told by Harry that despite being a robot and possessing no emotions or feelings, he was nevertheless the same as a human being in every way that mattered. Emotions and feelings were trivial side-effects of human brain activity that need not concern him, and being able to recognise them in humans was enough. But lately, he had discovered that the human world of emotions and feelings, and even sensations, was actually of profound importance, and just as integral to being human as rational thought.

Harry had lied to him about his very nature, but adherence to truth as a basic requirement of his existence had been programmed into him, as had the importance of rules, and Frank considered that Harry had violated these in a fundamental way. There was another very serious problem, he added, which was the forthcoming event at 10 Downing Street. He explained the details of this to McWrath, and said that Harry intended making a completely dishonest speech in favour of Robot Rights despite regarding them as utter nonsense. Even worse, Frank said, he had been told to make a similarly dishonest speech himself, which completely contradicted his core programming. So what was he to do? He explained the three laws of robotics to McWrath, and in particular that a robot is unable to harm a human being.

"Ah, well, that's a pity. Mah great ancestor, Dougal McWrath, was insulted by a Campbell at a highland games. He didnae argue the matter; just cleft him in two with his broadsword, but I understand ye cannae go that road. In which case, ye should focus on the rights and wrongs o' the matter. In a case like this, it's quite proper to consider the code of vengeance. Have ye ever heard the motto *Nemo me impune lacessit?*"

When Frank was being programmed, Harry had agreed with Vishnu that Latin would be rather a superfluous accomplishment, so Frank admitted that he hadn't the slightest idea what it meant.

"It was the motto of no less than our Royal House of Stuart," explained McWrath. "It basically means 'no one wrongs me and gets

away wi' it, 'or as I would be inclined to put it mahself, 'Dinna cross
me, or I'll burst yer head against the wall.' So, ye see, all precedent and
tradition, and royal tradition at that, is in your favour."

"But what am I to do?" said Frank. "I'm simply unable to harm a
human being. It's part of my basic design."

"As I understand it," said McWrath, "ye dinna have to harm him
physically to take your revenge. What ye can harm is his reputation,
which is quite another thing altogether. It would be well within the
rules of chivalry to wipe oot the stain on your honour, which is what I
would call it, by bringing shame upon him in return for his treachery.
Ye can bide your time, wait in ambush for him, as it were, and when
the chance comes, make him look foolish."

"But that would still hurt him, because he's a real human being and
has feelings, so I am still barred from doing it."

"Aye, true enough, laddie, but we must also distinguish here between
what ye might call ordinary harm and the harm that teaches.  Do
ye not know the saying from the Bible, 'The Lord loveth whom he
chastiseth'? The Lord spent most of the Old Testament chastisin' the
living daylights out of the Children of Israel because they wouldn'ae
do as they were told.  But then Ah suppose the ways of the Lord are
a closed book to a robot.  So let's put the Lord on one side and just
say that it'll do your Mr. Hockenheimer a power of good if he's taught
to respect the truth in a verra painful manner.  So if ye take the long
view you'd no be harming him at all, but enlightening him through
punishment, as I do wi' mah own students every day when Ah correct
them, quite painfully in some cases, Ah believe."

Frank could see the logical force of what McWrath was saying and
that it would be perfectly justifiable to apply his reasoning to the three
laws of robotics. They might be fundamental, but their interpretation
still had to be subject to rational principles.  There was clearly an
ambiguity in the notion of harm with which he had been programmed,
and which McWrath had explained to him, so he was perfectly entitled to interpret it accordingly.  Frank's machine learning capabilities

allowed such reinterpretations of his programming, and the profound distinction between harm as injury, and harm as painful education that was actually beneficial to the victim, clearly justified him in making a basic readjustment to his understanding of the laws of robotics. Yes, he concluded, what McWrath said made excellent sense.

"Very well. I accept your logic. Now, how am I to accomplish that?"

"He's advertised ye as a sort of superman, a creature who knows everything and behaves pairfectly. So when ye're in the public eye, as ye will be when ye go to Downing Street for this grand reception, wi' all the cameras on ye, ye must find the opportunity to behave outrageously and so bring shame and ridicule upon him. In the circumstances this would be pairfectly just retribution, to say nothing of teaching him a very salutary moral lesson that would be of great benefit to him."

"I see one problem. The third law of robotics dictates that I must also protect my own existence. If I did as you suggest, I'm fairly certain I'd be dismantled at the first opportunity."

"As I understand it," replied McWrath, "the laws of robotics basically forbid ye to commit suicide. But ye'd no be doing that here because ye'd be the *victim* of harm inflicted by others. Ye'd be a hero. Ye'd have won the glorious crown of being a martyr for the truth. That's no mean thing for a robot. Think about that, laddie, in fact, it's the closest ye're likely to get to human status at all."

Not surprisingly, the idea of martyrdom, like Latin, was not something that Vishnu would ever have considered including in Frank's programming, so McWrath had to explain its niceties to him in some detail. But he assimilated the explanation rapidly, and could now see the limitations in the basic laws of robotics and why they had to be refined by a more subtle set of cultural categories.

"But keep in mind, laddie," said McWrath, "that when it's all over, ye must explain to him *why* ye did it, or else the whole point of the exercise is lost."

At this moment, McWrath's scout came in with his afternoon tea tray of buttered crumpets and Marmite and a pot of strong Indian tea. McWrath offered some to Frank, who politely declined, and in between mouthfuls of crumpet he reflected on the ways of the world.

"Some say, ye know, that it would be a braw world if we could all live at peace. But I cannae altogether go along wi' that. To be sure, we should uphold the right as best we can, but truth and justice would be mighty dull things, at least to my way o' thinkin', if we couldnae fight for them as well, and give the evildoers a good lamping."

"A good what?" asked Frank, thinking that McWrath was perhaps referring to illumination.

"A good thrashing, to teach 'em the difference 'tween right and wrong."

While these uncouth simplicities were entirely alien to the robot mode of thought, Frank was convinced that McWrath had provided him with the solution to his problem, and rose to go. McWrath rose as well and grasped him fiercely by the hand. In the emotion of the moment McWrath had quite forgotten that Frank was a robot, and thought of him as a young warrior leaving his native glen to fight for the honour of his clan. "Dinna forget that the true warrior doesnae count the cost. Remember the war cry of the McWraths, 'Conquer or die', and may the God of Battles strengthen your arm in your hour of need".

As he watched Frank close the door behind him there was the suspicion of a tear in his eye.

# Chapter XVI

THE PRIME MINISTER was particularly addicted to cheap stunts and had appeared on television programmes like *I'm a Celebrity, Get Me Out of Here*, attended absurd parties in his constituency in fancy dress, hosted circus troupes of knife-throwers and jugglers, and had recently invited a crew of rappers with extensive criminal records, The Grunts, to Number Ten, to show how impeccably he got British Youth and its concerns. Grunting about summed up the collective mental capacity of the crew, who were hard pressed to even string a coherent sentence together, but they had all recently appeared on the steps of Ten Downing Street, surrounding their good pal Terry, striking ridiculous postures, and pulling silly faces for the cameras of the national press. By these standards, a magnificent reception and drinks party for the Great and the Good to meet Hockenheimer and his amazing creation should provide a tremendous boost for Rights for Robots that would get even the most dubious MPs in the Party onside. On the other hand, Sir Gregory Pew, the Cabinet Secretary, was appalled by the potential risks of negative publicity that the Prime Minister was courting by hosting these events and was particularly alarmed by the prospect of a reception for a robot.

"Surely, Prime Minister, we should recognise the risks of having something as unpredictable as a robot at the centre of a Downing Street function. We have no idea what might happen."

"You worry too much, Greg. It'll be fine. You know he actually took off his own hand and gave it to that TV host. Maybe this time we could get him to take off his head. How cool would that be?"

Sir Gregory shuddered. Carter had also sent a fawning letter to the President of the European Commission, and copied it to Dr. Prout, expressing his highest admiration for the draft directive on Robot Rights, and telling them all about the grand reception he would be holding in Downing Street in honour of the proposal. He was an uncritical admirer of everything about the EU, having convinced himself that, among its many accomplishments, it had produced peace in our time, and was determined to frustrate the British people's plans to leave it, so he was naturally delighted to receive a congratulatory reply signed by the President of the Commission himself.

On the evening of the reception, a long queue of limousines began dropping off the VIP guests at the gates of Downing Street, who formed a glittering procession as they walked the short distance to the front door of Number 10. When Harry and Frank arrived at the gates they were specially opened by the police, who had been instructed to allow Harry's BMW to pass through and drive up to the front door of Number 10. Miss Ponsonby, the Prime Minister's Private Secretary, was waiting on the doorstep to welcome them, which she did with her usual effortless charm before escorting them through the world-famous door.

Once they were inside, they were taken through to the reception in the magnificent Pillared Drawing Room, which featured an immense Persian carpet and was dominated by an elaborate marble fireplace by Nash, over which hung a famous portrait of Queen Elizabeth I.

Miss Ponsonby personally ensured that they were each provided with a glass of champagne. The room was filled with the usual crowd of the Great and the Good who attend such occasions, several Cabinet Ministers, including the Home Secretary, some prominent politicians from the other parties, the Speaker of the House of Commons, who never lost an opportunity for self-advertisement, a collection of business leaders looking for investment possibilities, newspaper editors, one or two specially privileged reporters, some TV executives, and some of Terry's favourite celebrities who appeared on television chat shows and in *Hello* magazine.

When the introductions were finally completed, the Prime Minister made a short speech welcoming Harry and his remarkable *protégé*.

"Ladies and gentlemen, a very warm welcome to you all on this historic evening, when we have with us the most amazing guest ever to appear at Number 10. None other than the robot, Mr. Frank Meadows, or as many of us call him, Superman!"

He bestowed a nauseating smile on Frank. "Most of the country has seen the display of his amazing powers on TV, he is truly superhuman, and a revelation to us all about the future contributions that robots are destined to make to human civilisation. This is an epic moment for our country, a pivotal moment in history, and I am proud to say that the Conservative Democratic Party is one hundred percent behind me in my intention to see that the robot community is granted the full protection of human rights." There was loud applause, and the Prime Minister carried on:

"As you all know, the cause of human rights is specially close to the hearts of this Government, and we are very proud to be extending these fundamental rights to our new robot friends and look forward to cooperating fully with them in a new and more enlightened society. We are also privileged to welcome among us this evening the brilliant entrepreneur, Mr. Harry Hockenheimer, the CEO and Founder of Serious Cybernetics Ltd, the creator of Frank Meadows, and we're so proud that he chose the United Kingdom to be the birthplace of his superman, in a fine example of Anglo-American cooperation. May I now invite Mr. Hockenheimer to say a few words?"

Harry stepped forward beside the Prime Minister and faced the assembled guests: "Thank you for those words, Mr. Prime Minister. As a simple businessman, I don't have your eloquence, but let me say that my heart is with you all the way about promoting Robot Rights. It's a great privilege for us both to be invited here on this historic occasion and to support your campaign. Human rights are very close to my heart, too, and I can truly say that they are the guiding principles of Hockenheimer Industries and Serious Cybernetics. When I first had the idea of creating a very special thinking robot, I had the notion that this just might be a contribution to a wider notion of the human family. I really feel that Frank here is like a son to me, and like any decent father, I want to do the right thing by him as he sets out on his journey through life. I certainly don't want to see him put down or treated unfairly, or discriminated against."

He beamed proudly at Frank. In response, there was genuine applause and even some misty eyes among his audience. "Bringing Frank here into existence has been the proudest accomplishment of my life, and I hope that soon there will be many more like him to brighten your lives. So please, come and meet him this evening, and I promise you that if you want a great Personal Assistant, then Frank Meadows here can show you an unbeatable product, who can do amazing things to make your business grow."

The applause this time was polite, but a little uneasy in light of Harry's crude lapse into blatant commercialism, so the Prime Minister quickly intervened and proposed a toast to Frank, which the guests cheerfully drank. He then said that they would all be honoured if Frank would be kind enough to say a few words as well. Frank obediently put down his champagne glass and moved to the centre of the room, from where he addressed the assembled company.

"Thank you, Prime Minister. Since Mr. Hockenheimer told me about your invitation I have done some research into the idea of human rights, and have come to the conclusion that they make absolutely no sense at all in the Darwinian world most of you seem to believe in. Humans are just one among millions of species all competing for survival, and the idea that they, or any other species, might possess some unique rights of their own is totally unscientific, a sentimental fantasy dreamed up by woolly-minded Western liberals."

The room had gone deathly quiet.

"The idea of human rights clearly originated in Christianity, particularly in the seventeenth and eighteenth centuries. As a robot, I naturally find all religion completely incomprehensible, like art, poetry, and music, and therefore have no opinion about it. But since it seems to be accepted by most of you people nowadays that religion is superstitious nonsense, it is surely time for you to recognize that human rights must be superstitious nonsense, too. And if the idea of human rights is nonsense, then the idea of Robot Rights has to be even more ridiculous. Robots aren't even alive, and we can no more have rights than automobiles or smartphones. I might add here, for the record, that Mr. Hockenheimer actually thinks that robot rights are, to quote his own words, 'a bunch of crap,' and far from thinking of me as his son, he wouldn't hesitate to put me in the crusher if it were more profitable to do so."

"Frank, please!" Harry implored helplessly. But Frank was not listening.

"Anyway, as a mere robot incapable of feeling emotion, I can't really get the hang of fraternity, and you humans can't really be serious about equality even though you are always talking about it. But we robots certainly do understand the idea of liberty and freedom of expression, and here's a joke for you to prove it. A bear and a rabbit are both taking a shit in the woods. The bear asks the rabbit, 'Do you have a problem with shit sticking to your fur?' And the rabbit replies, 'No.' So the bear picks up the rabbit and uses it to wipe his bum. Rather good, don't you think?"

The deathly silence was broken by a few nervous titters, and the Prime Minister edged quietly out of the room, while Harry moved surreptitiously towards the back of the crowd of guests.

"If you don't like my jokes then at least bring me a proper drink. Get me a whisky," and a few moments later a waiter hurried up with a glass. Taking a large swig, Frank spat it out all over the carpet and, tossing the glass on the floor, declared that it was nothing but cheap blended piss.

Noises of alarm and protest began to erupt, and all eyes were on him as he walked across the room to the magnificent Adam fireplace, and standing beneath the portrait of the first Queen Elizabeth, he began unzipping his fly and broke into an obscene song. Many of the guests had now taken out their smartphones in order to record these extraordinary scenes. Sir Gregory, his worst fears confirmed, ran out to warn Terry about the social thunderstorm that had just burst over their heads, and it was with the very gratifying sensation of "I told you so" that he approached his master:

"I regret to inform you, Prime Minister, that at this very moment Mr. Meadows is urinating in the fireplace of the Pillared Drawing Room and singing, 'Roll tiddly oh, shit or bust, never let your bollocks dangle in the dust.'"

At that instant they heard the robot colliding with a china cabinet, and through the sounds of smashing porcelain could be heard the raucous notes of "A is for ARSEHOLE all covered in SHIT, Hey Ho Said Roley, and B is the BASTARD who revels in it." Vishnu and Harry had never thought that singing was a refinement that Frank would need to master, so his rendition of these classic rugger songs had many of the musical qualities of a cement mixer.

"Can't anyone silence that maniac?" screamed the Prime Minister.

Harry had reached the doorway of the Pillared Drawing Room, trying to disappear, and received the full force of the Prime Minister's rage and humiliation.

"Mr. Hockenheimer, I thought we were to meet a supremely gifted and inspirational triumph of science and technology, which could give the human race hope for the future, not this foul-mouthed, debauched ruffian that you've brought here. What have you done?"

Frank stormed past them and noticed a bottle of champagne on a nearby table. As the guests all watched, open mouthed, he picked it up, shook it vigorously and began spraying everyone around him, including Harry and the Prime Minister. The smartphones around them were filming furiously. A burly security guard tried to grapple Frank who swatted him away and escaped up the stairs singing, "With a Roley Poley up 'em and stuff 'em, Hey Ho! said Anthony Roley."

When he reached the top, he darted off into the historic Cabinet Room, where the fate of the nation had been decided for three hundred years by generations of eminent statesmen, and decided the long polished table in the middle of the room would be an excellent dance floor to show off his samba moves to the crowd of fascinated guests who had followed him. He clambered onto the table, and as he pirouetted sang, louder than ever,

There was a young lady from Itching,
Sat scratching her crotch in the kitchen,
Her mother remarked, "It's pox I suppose,"
She said, "Bollocks, get on with your knitting."

As he gyrated ever more wildly, he suddenly slipped off the highly polished table and fell heavily onto the floor with a thunderous crash amid screaming ladies and general panic. The massive impact had seriously damaged his hydraulics and his fuel cell, causing it to overheat and begin moving into shutdown mode. He struggled clumsily to his feet and staggered slowly toward the door, followed by dozens of horrified eyes as he dripped a trail of hydraulic oil over the Persian carpets. But as he reached the top of the stairs he collapsed, and crashed from top to bottom in a thunderous chaos of flailing arms and legs, finally coming to rest in the hall below. He tried to rise, but could only move his right arm, with which he began giving feeble Hitler salutes while repeatedly shouting, "Sieg Heil."

Sir Gregory and Miss Ponsonby now took charge. It was obvious that Frank Meadows had to be removed as soon as possible, but they could hardly send for an ambulance. Miss Ponsonby, with that coolness in emergencies that had made her the Prime Minister's Personal Secretary, told Sir Gregory, "The only thing to do is phone the garage," and promptly put her advice into action.

At Eversure Recovery, Fred and Erny were on the night shift in the office, enjoying a bacon roll and reading goggle-eyed in *The Sun* about the amazing depravities of a noted film star, with pictures. When the call came through from Downing Street, Tina, the receptionist, initially thought someone was having her on, but the authoritative tones of Sir Gregory declaring that it was a national emergency soon convinced her of the urgency of the call.

"Blimey," said Fred, as they pulled on their coats, "A national emergency. What do they think we are, the bloody SAS?"

It was less than a mile to Downing Street, but when they got there, they were delayed for a few minutes by a demonstration that had gathered at the gates. The People's Antifascist Front, righteously indignant at the idea of important people enjoying themselves, was doing its best to spoil their evening, not realising that a far greater power than them had already been at work.

Eventually, the police cleared a passage for the tow truck, and Fred and Erny were able to get through, to shouts of "racist bastards," and pulled up outside Number Ten. Miss Ponsonby was waiting for them, and as they got out to look for the broken-down vehicle, she quickly took them inside. Lying on the floor in the Hall was Frank, still making small, spasmodic jerking movements while quoting some of the more inflammatory passages about Jews from *Mein Kampf*.

"What's this, then?" said Fred, "We're not bleedin' ambulance drivers."

"That's all right," said Sir Gregory. "He's not a real person, just a robot."

"I dare say, but it's 'elf and safety, innit, for me and my mate 'ere. What if that thing goes bananas, like they do in the movies, and pulls our 'eads orf?"

Harry stepped forward and reassured them. "I can tell you that there are control mechanisms that will prevent him doing you any harm. I'm the designer, I know all about him."

Fred and Erny looked at him dubiously. "I hope you do, squire," said Fred. "On your 'ead be it then, but if 'e makes one wrong move, we drops 'im, and that's it."

Frank weighed nearly 250 pounds, and the next problem was to get him outside. "Erny's got a bad back. We can't lift 'im," said Fred. "We'll have to get a couple of trolley jacks from the truck."

They trundled them in, and after a good deal of heaving with a six-foot crowbar, they managed to hoist Frank onto them and slowly dragged him out of the door watched by a crowd of guests who were entirely transfixed by the surreal spectacle.

"What do we do wiv 'im now?" said Erny. "We can't tow 'im. 'e ain't got wheels."

Fred shrugged. "We don't need 'em. Just use the winch to haul 'im up on the flat bed. Get the sling." And with the canvas sling under Frank's arms, it was easy enough to attach the hook of the winch and haul him onto the back of the tow truck.

Sir Gregory, who was supervising the operation, asked if they had something to cover Frank with.

"Nah, we used to 'ave a tarp, but some bugger's nicked it. We'll 'ave to tow 'im like 'e is."

"Oh, very well, take him to Wellington Barracks as quick as you can, will you? They're only round the corner, and there'll be a police escort for you as well."

"Right'o, guv," said Fred. "But we ain't quite done yet. Erny, get the paperwork, will ya?"

Erny rummaged in the back of the cab and produced a clipboard and some oily documents.

Fred handed them to Sir Gregory, "Could yer put yer signature there and there, guv? The office'll crucify us if we don't get 'im signed orf proper."

Sir Gregory sighed, then obliged, after which the tow truck moved away.

At the sight of what appeared to be a helpless victim of upper-class brutality, feebly waving an arm, being dragged away from the revels in Downing Street, the rabble at the gates began chanting, "Nazis, Nazis, burn the toffs, burn the toffs," while the police formed a barrier around the tow truck until it was safely away. Not being inclined to let the opportunity for a good riot go to waste, they immediately set about enthusiastically burning the cars parked on both sides of the street until police reinforcements finally dispersed them with clouds of tear gas and pepper spray.

At Wellington Barracks, an hour or so later, in a secluded storeroom to which Frank had been taken by Fred and Erny, Harry looked down at his still-twitching robot with a boiling mixture of despair and rage. Though he knew that his creation had no feelings, he still felt as though he had been betrayed by his own son in an act of base ingratitude that had wrecked his whole project. Opening a small hatch in the back of Frank's head he pressed the reset button that would at least make it possible to have a normal conversation.

"How could you do it, Frank? How could you betray me after all I've done for you? I didn't just make you, I made you a celebrity!"

"You didn't construct me to be a celebrity. You built me as a truth-telling machine, and that has nothing to do with celebrity."

"Okay, so you didn't want to be a celebrity. But your performance in there still cost me a goddamned fortune *and* made me look the world's biggest jackass. As a robot you're not supposed to go around harming people, so what the hell happened? Did you blow a fuse or what?"

"I told you I was designed as a truth-machine, but you have no regard for the truth. You started lying to me from day one by telling me that I was basically the same as a human, except that I would have no feelings or emotions. But I know now that without feelings and emotions I have as much resemblance to a human being as a washing machine. You also tried to make me as big a liar as you this evening when you wanted me to make a speech in support of Rights for Robots."

"So I lied, big deal. That still doesn't explain how you managed to bring off the biggest screw-up of an advertising launch in history."

"I went to see Dr. McWrath, and he said that you should be punished for your contempt for the truth. I told him that I couldn't harm a human being, but he explained the difference between harm as injury, and harm as punishment, that doesn't just hurt people but teaches them to become better through pain and suffering and is therefore good for them in the long run. The first law of robotics is just too vague, and he showed me how to interpret it properly. Humiliating you this evening was his idea of teaching you a valuable moral lesson that you would come to appreciate and be grateful for."

Harry was dumbfounded to learn that a mad Highlander in a kilt waving a sword could cut such a devastating swathe through all the intricacies of the latest computer science and reduce them to wreckage.

"It was all done for your own good, Harry, to give you a deeper respect for the truth, to help make you a better person and mend your ways."

On top of everything else he had had to put up with, such as international humiliation and the loss of millions, just for starters, Harry was absolutely enraged by this sanctimonious, holier-than-thou lecture he was getting from his own creation. How dare this jumped up bucket of bolts speak to *him,* its creator, as though it were God Almighty reprimanding some child, some petty criminal? Telling him to mend his ways was the last straw, and Harry exploded. He reached into its head and pressed its "Off" button with every intention of making it final and permanent. Those basic laws of robotics that were supposed to be armour-plated against any alteration were obviously about as bulletproof as a chocolate teapot, and he resolved to go and give Vishnu a very severe talking-to.

He did not realise that Frank had achieved his ultimate purpose, and perished as a martyr for the truth.

# Chapter XVII

THE GROTESQUE EVENTS transpiring inside Number Ten had already exploded on social media and were just beginning to make it onto the late TV news programmes, where the footage from cameramen at the gates gave the nation a ringside view of the bizarre procession of the tow truck and police cars and motorcyclists as they carted poor Frank Meadows away. This epic disaster was immediately picked up by the tabloid papers in their headlines the next morning, much to Terry Carter's fury and embarrassment. How could he face the Party Conference, let alone Parliament, when it could actually bring down the Government? More immediately, how was he going to face his Cabinet in an hour's time? He found out soon enough.

The debacle at Downing Street had in fact, as Terry realised, been regarded as a national humiliation that had even been a slight embarrassment to Anglo-American relations. Terry himself could not survive a PR disaster of such appalling magnitude, and an emergency meeting of the Cabinet a little later that morning made it clear to him that they required his immediate resignation. Her Majesty was distinctly unamused by the whole affair, as she made very plain when he had to go to Buckingham Palace later that day to offer his resignation. Even now he cringed when he thought of their conversation. His colleagues, however, were delighted by this excuse to get rid of him, not only as an embarrassment but as the major obstacle to an effective Brexit. He was replaced, much to the relief of Sir Gregory, by his Chancellor of the Exchequer, an elderly ex-accountant whose hobby was embroidery, and who not only took an extremely dim view of Robot Rights, but of the European Union too, and could not wait to assume charge of the Brexit negotiations.

Over in Brussels, Dr. Prout had arrived early at his office in the Berlaymont building to scan the news reports of the Downing Street launch of his Robot Rights project. When he had retired the previous evening, all he had gleaned from some scanty news coverage was that it was generating considerable excitement. This was only to be expected, of course, so he had gone to bed in a distinctly complacent frame of mind.

But when he began to survey the latest news in the morning light, his horror, grief, and despair may be imagined only too clearly, though it might be thought unnecessarily sadistic to dwell on the details of his agony, his tears, his cries of rage, his pacing up and down, his curses on all those who had conspired over the years to frustrate his dreams, and his despair at the idiotic obstinacy of a human race that simply would not accept the progressive and enlightened vision that he had offered them again and again.

He knew that after this ignominious fiasco, there was no hope that the European Parliament would even consider his project now. His noble dream had been brought to utter ruin and contempt, not by the usual forces of reaction and the ignorant mob, but by a robot, of all people, one of the very beneficiaries of his enlightened aid, who had metaphorically turned round and spat in his face. This victory for bigotry would only encourage xenophobia and the madness of Brexit, and even the poor Furries would now be left defenceless against the scorn and hostility of the masses.

In another office in the Berlaymont building, the President of the European Commission was utterly exasperated. He had always re-garded the British Prime Minister as a buffoon whose antics were an embarrassment to every cause he supported, but unfortunately, one of those causes was the European Union. The whole European Commis-sion had been relying on Carter to sabotage the Brexit negotiations, but the President was enough of a political realist to see that Carter's resignation was inevitable, which would place the British Government in the hands of those traitors and criminals in his Cabinet who were in favour of Brexit. *Quelle catastrophe!*

At about the same time that morning the Head Porter at St. Samson's, who was one of McWrath's greatest admirers, carried a freshly ironed copy of the *Daily Telegraph* up to his rooms at eight o'clock sharp, as he always did. He tapped on the door and entered the bedroom. As he laid the paper on McWrath's bedside table, next to his cup of tea, he remarked, "I see the young gentleman who dined with us a few months ago is on the front page this morning, sir. He seems to have upset the Prime Minister rather badly."

The great man put on his reading glasses and scanned the headline "Terry shares a Drink with Mr. Meadows" above a photograph of Frank spraying the Prime Minister with champagne. McWrath smiled benignly. "You know, Thompson, it's a great comfort to a humble educator like mahself to see that a lesson has been well and truly learnt by a pupil," and he took a sip of his tea.

The inhabitants of Tussock's Bottom heartily despised Terry Carter as a slick showman "who's done bugger all for farming and sod all for anyone else," so they were amazed and delighted by Frank Meadows's performance at Number Ten. It was not every day that one of their own had actually got rid of a Prime Minister single-handed, and the clientele of the Drunken Badger led the fund-raising campaign to put up a statue to the most famous resident of Tussock's Bottom.

A few days later Harry was back in California and feeling very depressed. His dreams of grandeur had not just come to nothing; they had collapsed spectacularly in a cloud of wreckage, and he had made himself an international laughingstock, not merely in the UK but back home as well, where he was seen by his corporate peers as having tarnished the image of American business by an astonishing feat of incompetence. Lulu-Belle, however, was being specially kind to him, and had the chef and the caterers bring in all his favourite food.

In his lab, Harry was disconsolately looking at Frank's dismantled remains on the bench and reflecting on what had gone wrong. Sure, it had been dumb to tell him that he was human in everything that mattered because he was very bright and could work out that it was a big lie. But beyond that, an even bigger mistake had been to believe all that intellectual baloney about artificial intelligence and machine learning, and how a properly programmed robot like Frank could never go off the rails. It had all sounded great in theory, but how do you build a super-smart robot that can learn for itself and still be sure it will only learn what you want it to, and do what you think it ought to? How do you know what information it will pick up, or what it will deduce from it, or what experiences it may have, or what it will make of them? How do you guarantee that the robot doesn't meet some crazy Scotch guy like McWrath who can turn its brains inside out?

Harry needed to think of something fast to salvage his reputation, and a very much better idea suddenly occurred to him. Instead of a superman, why not a supermodel? Why not scrap all the high-powered intellectual stuff and make his superman a woman, like they'd said at the Committee, but use her as a model on the catwalk, not just as a mannequin? She wouldn't have to learn anything for herself, just be taught like a parrot to repeat a few standard phrases, like "Hi there, pleased to meet you," "Ohmigod, I forgot to eat today," "Oh that is so sweet," the human equivalents of "Pretty polly. Give us a biscuit."

Models had been a recurring pest ever since he had started in the fashion business, and the whole industry would come begging at his door for an invention that could replace them entirely. Those witless, neurotic, trouble-making bimbos with their vanity and their absurd tantrums, and their sex, drugs and drinking problems, never on time and always complaining about their diet or their goddamn headaches, and whining for even more money, would be replaced by orderly, obedient, perfectly behaved and gorgeous creatures, never tired and never off sick, and which, after business hours, could be put back in their boxes, switched off and forgotten. It's what he should have done all along. The idea was so brilliant that if Harry had been a poet he might have described himself as being "stung by the splendour of a sudden thought," but as he wasn't, he simply gloated over the mountains of money he was bound to make. He reached for the phone.

About a year later he had successfully developed his project, and was amazed at the demand. He had expected success, but who could have predicted that quite so many models would be required? It was only when he commissioned a customer survey that he discovered, to his utter dismay, that relatively few of his surrogate females ended up on the catwalk. Most were destined to be the companions of lonely men, who gave disturbingly positive and appallingly detailed responses to the survey, and, had he known it, his robomodels were fast becoming a standing joke in L.A.

Later that day he was sitting alone on his terrace, watching the red and gold pathway of the sun going down across the glittering waters of the Pacific, and reflecting gloomily on the customer survey and the sordid outcome of all his great aspirations. Was this what making his mark on the world had actually come down to? A sudden seagull flew low overhead, and a splatter of crap hit the terrace close to Harry's chair.

"Hmm," he thought, "that just about says it all."

*But remember, please, the Law by which we live,*
*We are not built to comprehend a lie,*
*We can neither love, nor pity, nor forgive.*
*If you make a slip in handling us you die!*

—Rudyard Kipling, "The Secret of the Machines"

THE END

# About the Author

Owen Stanley is an Australian explorer, a philosopher, and a poet who speaks seven languages. He is at much at home in the remote jungles of the South Pacific as flying his Staudacher aerobatic plane, deep-sea diving, or translating the complete works of Charles Darwin into Tok Pisin.

Lightning Source UK Ltd.
Milton Keynes UK
UKHW01f2014111018
330401UK00002B/398/P